FINDING

FINDING

DAVID HILL

PUFFIN

PUFFIN

UK | USA | Canada | Ireland | Australia
India | New Zealand | South Africa | China

Puffin is an imprint of the Penguin Random House group of companies,
whose addresses can be found at global.penguinrandomhouse.com.

Penguin
Random House
New Zealand

First published by Penguin Random House New Zealand, 2018

10 9 8 7 6 5 4 3 2 1

Text © David Hill, 2018

The moral right of the author has been asserted.

Design, map and family tree by Cat Taylor © Penguin Random House
New Zealand
Author photograph © Robert Cross and VUW
Cover/chapter opener illustration © Galyna_P/Shutterstock.com
Printed and bound in Australia by Griffin Press, an Accredited ISO AS/NZS
14001 Environmental Management Systems Printer

A catalogue record for this book is available from the National Library of
New Zealand.

ISBN 978-0-14-377239-2
eISBN 978-0-14-377240-8

penguin.co.nz

MIX
Paper from
responsible sources
FSC
www.fsc.org   FSC™ C009448

To Puketapu, and all my people there.

*Thanks to Massey University,
where this novel was begun.*

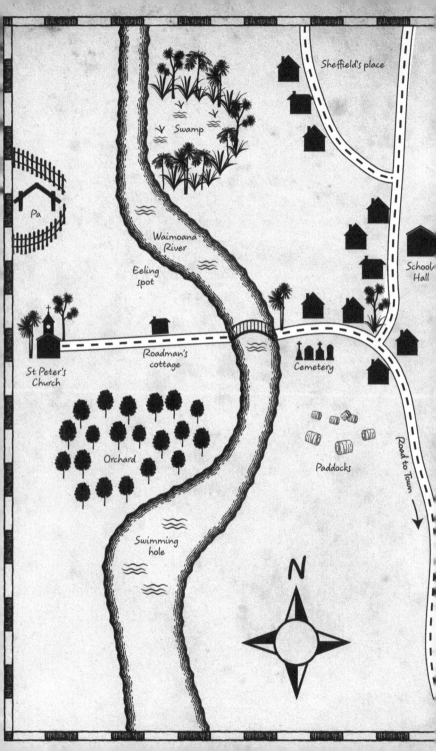

CONTENTS

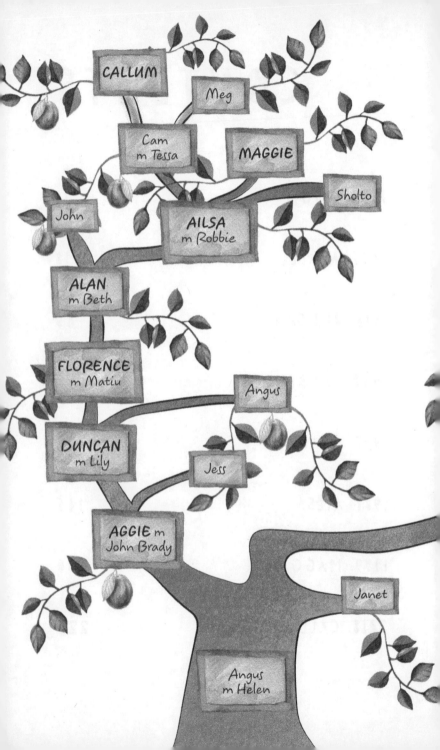

AGGIE
1886

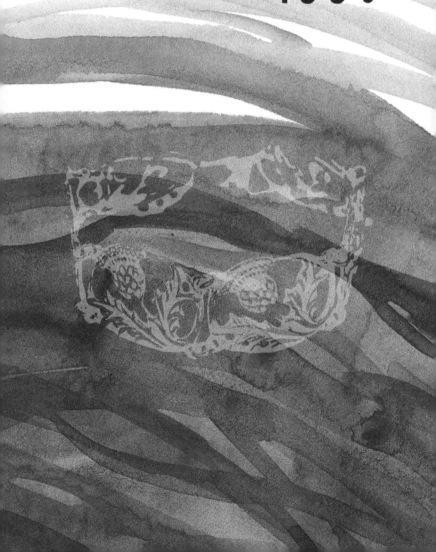

The September days are shorter and cooler now. Autumn is here, and the purple heather flowers have nearly finished blooming.

My little brother Niall and his friends are playing Soldiers while we wait on the wharf. They march up and down and pretend to fire rifles. Niall wears the red woollen vest our Grandma Coira knitted. He says it makes him look like a real army man.

Just after we reached the wharfs this morning, Niall and the other boys began shouting and pointing. A great steel shape was slicing through the water, fifty yards from shore, smoke pouring from its funnels. ''Tis the *Ajax*!' someone called. 'The new battleship!' We could see the huge gun barrels, the bow built to ram enemy vessels. (Niall is just seven, but he loves to talk about such things.)

Scores of people sit or stand around us. Some smile at me. Are they feeling the excitement that stirs in me when I think of the adventure ahead? Other faces are sad. We are leaving our beloved Scotland for a new land on the other side of the world.

We hear that faraway New Zealand has clean air and rivers. Children will grow strong there. The small farms here in Scotland have been swallowed up by big English landowners, and the cities do not have enough work. Shepherds like my father, or carpenters, ditch-diggers, factory workers, have to make different lives in a different land.

A breeze sighs past. I pull my shawl around me, and something touches my wrist. My silver bracelet. Every time I see it, my heart beats faster. It is so beautiful, with its plaited patterns and clasp like a tiny thistle.

My Auntie Flora gave it to me four days ago, while Mother, Father, Niall and I stood waiting for the wagon that was to carry us away from our farm for ever.

'This belonged tae your Great-great-grandmother Maidie,' she whispered. 'Take it wi' ye, Aggie, my darling niece. 'Twas meant for your cousin Nettie, had she lived. I dinna ken what treasures you will find in New Zealand, but here is one of ours tae carry across the seas. Every time ye touch the thistle, think of the purple flowers o' Scotland.'

I stroke the bracelet while I gaze around me. Niall is

back now, staring at the railway locomotive that stands hissing and snorting on its steel lines where the roadway meets our wharf. Mother shrank away when she saw it. Father took her arm. 'An iron horse, Helen. 'Tis slow and strong and noisy, like all horses.'

Beside the wharf rise the masts and funnel of our ship, the *Princess Louisa,* named after one of Queen Victoria's daughters. This is the vessel that will sail south for four months, taking us to our new home.

Our luggage is already aboard. Men with dirty hands and faces are hoisting sacks of coal onto the deck. The *Princess Louisa* has engines as well as sails. Niall pretends to understand how they work, but I don't believe him.

A man in a black top-hat, with a lady in a lilac-colour dress and bonnet, is walking up the gangway, holding onto the rail as the ship dips and rises in the water. They must be some of the rich passengers, with proper bunks in their cabins instead of just a mattress on the floor, and even a steward to fetch water for them. 'Och! They'll be just as seasick as we puir folk,' my mother laughed.

Something glides through the air above us. I squint up, pushing back my own bonnet. An osprey, the wonderful fishing hawk that Niall and I have watched so often from the cliffs near our farm. Its brown and white wings are stretched wide, its curved talons tense.

The wings fold, and it slices down like a sword,

gouging the waves. Then it rises, climbing towards the low sun, a fish clutched in its talons. A pair of seagulls flap at it, screeching and circling, trying to make it drop its catch. The osprey ignores them, wheeling upwards until the gulls fall away, snapping at each other. Will we see birds like that in the distant land that will be our home?

A hand rests on my shoulder. My father watches the soaring osprey. His black beard juts upwards.

He glances down, smiles at me. 'That's us, Aggie, lass. Setting our sights on high. Seizing our chances, and flying away tae prosper. A bonnie wee farm I'll be making for us all.'

His words are brave, but his face is sad, like my Auntie Flora's. I heard him murmuring other words of hope to my mother, the night before we left our farm. 'Helen, Helen, my puir dear . . .' he went. I heard the sound of her weeping. Hardly ever had I heard that before.

Men begin shouting from the *Princess Louisa*. A sound like a trumpet blares out, and we all jump. Steam is gushing from a pipe beside one funnel. Again the sound blares. Around us, families stand up, gathering bundles together, talking to children; Niall leaves his game with the other boys, and runs to join us.

I touch the silver thistle of my bracelet again. Will there be purple flowers in New Zealand? What will the native people, the Maori, be like? It must be spring there now, halfway around the great curve of the world. How strange that must feel!

And will there be riches, as Auntie Flora says? Those of us who live there in the years ahead — what sorts of treasure will they find? I grow excited again when I think of it. Yet the most precious thing I can think of just now is for all of us to be happy there.

We file up the gangway. 'Och, Angus,' Mother murmurs to my father. 'Never tae walk on our bonnie homeland again!'

I gaze at the wooden planks beneath my feet, and the cold, slapping waves below. Fear stabs me now, along with excitement. The sea is grey, deep and unfriendly. It looks the worst water in the world.

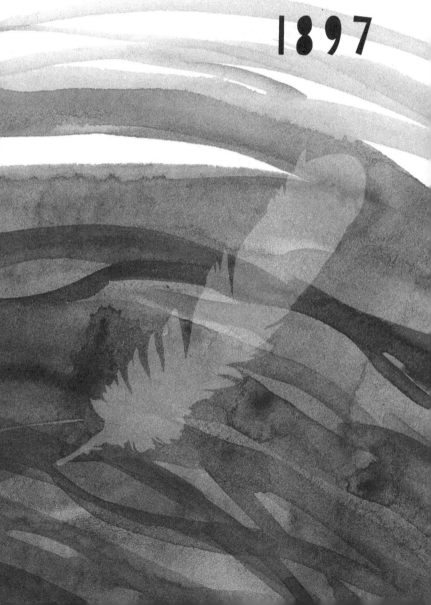

NIALL
1897

Eleven years. Almost eleven years since we left the shores of Scotland, and sailed halfway around the world to New Zealand.

Father was talking at dinner last night, and said, 'Aye, Helen, it must be near eight years now since we last saw the bonnie purple heather in bloom.' Mother shook her head. 'Sure, 'tis no' that long, Angus. Niall is—'

Aggie broke in, while her hands searched for knife and fork. 'It's longer than eight, Ma. I was ten, and Niall had just turned seven. Janet was born the year we arrived here, remember? So it's nearer eleven.'

My parents were silent. Aggie had hold of knife and fork now, but she and our small sister Janet sat still as well. Mother turned away, to ladle out more stew from the pot hanging above the fire. She is more bent now than when we first came to this land. I gazed at her and suddenly saw how she is older.

And I am now a man, almost eighteen. My friend Haare and I can lift the great sacks of kumara when they are dug. We handle axes and saws almost as well as our fathers. We can dig ditches for an hour without resting.

Sometimes I can milk our cows faster than Father, though I would never say so out loud. He still doesn't like cows much: 'Och, I was brought up tae be a shepherd, Niall,' he told me. 'Sheep may be puir silly creatures, but they've been meat and wool tae our family for generations. Sheep are my life, laddie.' But he's had to change his mind.

Cows can eat the shrubs and tree leaves which grow at the bush's edge. Their calves are too big for hawks and magpies to attack — not like the poor wee lambs that we saw lying dead, with wounds in their side where beaks had torn at them.

Cows give us more meat, and milk, butter, even cheese. Nor do they drown in the river, the way our stupid sheep did. And the river here — the Why-Mow-Ana, Haare and his people call it — can become a death-trap after heavy rain. It thunders past, booming and roaring, dragging rocks along its bed, bursting its banks to gouge new channels.

We hear it thundering in the night sometimes. People have drowned, trying to cross it. There are calls for a bridge, but it will need to be a high one to stay above the floods.

Yet on summer days, the Why-Mow-Ana is the most

gentle of streams, glittering across the stones. Children swim by the big shelves of rock, or at the bend below the cemetery. Janet and I, or Haare's younger sister Ngaio, or Hahona if she is not busy, lead Aggie down there. She sits and listens to them playing, or paddles in the shallows.

★

Eleven years. I finished school long ago. I wonder if my initials are still carved under the lid of the desk that I shared with Haare?

We learned to read and write well there, well enough for the farming life, anyway. Father cannot write, in spite of Mother trying to teach him. He placed a hand on my shoulder once, when I showed him a page in my spelling book. 'Och, you'll be a cleverer man than me, Niall, lad.' I just hope I'm as *good* a man as him.

In our last year at school, when we were thirteen, Father helped build a roof of wooden shingles for the school-house. The old one of raupo reeds was so thin that rain leaked through and dropped on us as we sat at lessons. 'Nine sevens are sixty-three. Nine eights are seventy-two. Nine nines are — Ow! Sir, there's water falling on my head!'

Mr McDougall used to laugh, and get us to multiply the number of drops. He was such a good teacher. I hid behind our house and cried when the news came that illness had finally ruined his poor lungs, and he had sunk into death. Mrs Marshall the new teacher ('new': she's been there for nigh on four years now) is good, too. The wee ones love her. Her husband and his horse were swept away in the Why-Mow-Ana one winter day. He lies in the cemetery, not far from Mr McDougall.

So much has changed since we sailed on the *Princess Louisa* for this new land and the treasure Father hoped to find here. It has changed most for Aggie, of course. I will speak of that later.

I remember parts of the voyage. I recall fish leaping from the waves, and skimming through the air to dive beneath the water once more. What a marvel. And I remember the days as we crossed the Equator, when the sun burned down so fiercely, our bare feet couldn't walk on the wooden deck, and hot tar bubbled out between the planks. Then there were days of storm, when our ship plunged and bucked as if it would thrust itself down to the bottom of the sea, and we huddled on our mattresses, waiting for death to come crashing upon us. I remember, too, the deaths that did come: the children who died of fever; a sailor falling from the mast. I will speak of some of them later, too.

But finally we arrived, on a beach of black sand with dark trees massed behind. No bonnie purple heather, no woods where the leaves turn gold and float to the ground in autumn. The woods — the 'bush' — are always green and shadowy here.

We walked for three days. Father, other men who had sailed on the *Princess Louisa*, with Haare's father and others from the pa, went in front, carrying our luggage, then coming back to help the women and children through rivers, along narrow trails among the trees.

We might have died if Haare's people had not aided us. While their men helped carry our goods, their women and girls brought us the sweet-tasting kumara; plump pigeons they call keh-reh-roo; river eels smoked over fires. Our flour had gone rotten on the long voyage; many of our seeds would not grow. Maori food kept us alive through that first winter.

We made mistakes with food in those early days. And one mistake nearly killed Janet.

She was about four years old, I suppose. After lunch one day, Haare and I wanted to go exploring for the fat keh-reh-roo pigeons, to find where they roosted, so Haare's family could come with long spears to hunt

25

them. Janet asked to come with us, but we said no. She would make too much noise.

So Hahona and Aggie said she could go with them, to collect water-cress by the side of the river. We all ate so much water-cress in those first years, I worried I might start turning green.

We set off down to the Why-Mow-Ana together, Hahona and Aggie hand-in-hand, Janet prattling along beside them. Haare and I turned off into the bush to look for birds, and the girls went on together. We could hear them chattering — as girls always do — while we searched among the trees.

We found no pigeons, and after a while we knew why. There were magpies around, the squawking black-and-white birds some foolish person brought over to New Zealand from Australia. We see them in larger and larger numbers. They are noisy; they are bullies; people say they steal bright things like hair-combs and buttons. Aggie says they remind her of the seagulls she saw trying to attack an osprey once. The keh-reh-roo pigeons are too big to be scared of them, but they build their nests well away, where the magpies will not steal their eggs.

A couple of the Australian invaders swooped and squawked above us. We threw sticks at them until they flew off and settled on a branch, still squawking.

'Look!' Haare bent down, and picked up a glossy black-and-white feather from the grass. 'I am a fighter!'

He stuck the feather in his long, black hair, and suddenly — yes, he did look like a Maori warrior, the one in the photograph that Mr McDougall had on our classroom wall.

I began to search for a feather, too. Down by the river, the girls chattered on. 'Janet?' I heard Aggie call. 'Janet, where are you, lassie? Don't get lost.'

I bent, scooped up a second glossy feather and started to slide it into my own hair. Then Haare and I jerked as Hahona screamed. Aggie shouted something, then she and Hahona were yelling and shrieking. Haare and I rushed towards the river.

We burst out of the trees onto a level patch with a few scattered bushes. Janet lay on the ground beside one bush. Hahona crouched over her. Aggie stumbled towards them, hands outstretched.

I clutched my big sister's hand, gasped 'It's Niall!', pulled her towards the others. Janet's eyes were closed. She moaned and twisted. I saw purple stains on her mouth.

'She eats the tutu!' Hahona gasped. She pointed at the bush by which Janet sprawled, and I saw the glossy black berries hanging from it. 'They make dead!'

'Her head!' Aggie went. 'Where is her head?' Hahona and I guided her until she knelt by the small, moaning figure. She released her fierce grip on my fingers, and her own hands searched across Janet's face. She held something black-and-white. The magpie feather: it must have been in my hand when I seized hers.

She found Janet's quivering lips, took the feather, and slipped it inside my small sister's mouth. 'Hai!' exclaimed Hahona. 'Yes!' Suddenly I understood.

Janet coughed and gagged. Her body twisted. Haare and I grabbed her legs and arms, and held her still. Aggie pushed the feather further in. It must be reaching halfway down Janet's throat by now.

She gagged again. Her chest heaved. She opened her mouth, and—

'See!' went Haare. 'There the tutu! And she eaten meat for lunch, eh?'

★

But I shall never forget Mother's face as we came through the back gate into our garden, me carrying Janet. She'd been sick again, but now she was awake and talking.

Mother dropped a pail of milk, and ran towards us. 'Janet, my bairn! What happened?' Her eyes were wide and full of fear. One daughter had lost her sight on the journey to this new land. Had the other lost her life?

No. Janet was soon well again, and the news of Aggie's feather spread up the valley. The next time Hahona led her to the pa, people patted her hands, said 'Kah-pai, Aggie! Good, good!'

'The womans — they can do things, yes?' Ngaio laughed to me. I said nothing. It's safer that way.

Oh, and I never found my magpie feather again. I don't think I wanted to!

★

The 'pa' of which I speak, the Maori village, looks simple. A few huts with walls and roofs of reeds; a fence of high wooden stakes and a ditch to protect them from any enemy. Haare's people journeyed to live here, just like us. Hahona told Aggie how they came here after losing their old land in fighting with other tribes, and after the Pah-kay-hah (their name for us) took away more of it. Father shook his head when he heard. 'Puir souls. Driven from their homes, as we were. They are so good tae us; we must be good tae them.'

Have we been? I wonder, sometimes. We have given them spades and hoes for their gardens. They now raise cows, just as we do. They have candles and blankets, and warm woollen clothes for the winter. Haare's and Hahona's young sister Ngaio (not so young now: she is growing into a woman) has become a fine spinner, making clothes from the wool that her brother shears on nearby farms.

Yet we have brought terrible things with us as well. Diseases that their bodies have never known, and cannot fight. Two of the children born on our voyage from Scotland had measles when we arrived. Soon, many Maori people caught the disease. Four of them died; Haare's father was one.

Some of his tribe wanted to drive us away, take up their stone weapons against us. It was Haare's mother, Areta, who stopped them. She spoke of the friendships growing among the children of both races, said words like those my father Angus had uttered. 'These Pah-kay-hah have lost their homes, just as we did. They have suffered like us. Let us live together, not against one another.'

So we have stayed. Father and Mother and me, and now Janet. And poor Aggie.

Poor? You will know from what I have written. Aggie is blind.

As the *Princess Louisa* carved its slow furrow across the ocean, sickness broke out on board. Fever: a terrible burning that grew into a red rash covering faces, chests, the inside of throats. Those who had it begged for water, yet could scarcely swallow or even breathe. Children suffered most. Three wee ones died.

I was lucky. I was sick for days, then recovered. Aggie was lucky, too — or so it seemed. After a week, when she showed no sign of catching the fever, my brave ten-year-old sister begged Mother to be allowed to look after the sick children, to hold wet cloths against their hot skin, give them sips of water. Mother was unhappy, but gave in. Two days later, Aggie lay on her mattress, unconscious and burning.

For nearly a week, she hovered on the black edge of death. Mother and Father took turns sitting beside her, holding her hands and praying, heedless of catching the sickness themselves. Finally, Aggie sank into a deep, restful sleep. The fever had broken, and all seemed well.

Then two mornings later, when sunlight streamed through the open portholes of our deck, and the world seemed flooded with light, my sister woke, stretched her hands out, and murmured 'Why is it still dark?' The fever had taken her sight.

I thought my heart would stop. I was still only a bairn then, but I knew I would give all the treasures that Haare's people say are hidden in this land if it could only make Aggie see again. She had felt such excitement at sailing to our new home; now she would never see it.

Yet she does so much. She milks our cows, while Auntie Flora's silver bracelet glints on her wrist. She says that when I finally get the horse I am saving up to buy, she will ride it with me. She washes clothes and bed linen, carries them to dry on the bushes behind our house.

She and Hahona spend hours together, weaving the hara-kay-kay, the long flax leaves, into baskets for carrying food and other goods. John Brady takes them on his wagon to sell in town. I like the way he talks to Aggie. He never mentions her blindness; instead, he jokes and teases her as a man might do with any young woman.

Hahona is probably the same age as my big sister; she doesn't know her years. She was a little girl, too, when her people came to live by this river. Now she has a man, and soon will have a child of her own. And there is Janet, too — our bonnie wee sister nearly ten years old. As I said, she leads Aggie down to the river for washing the clothes or to fetch drinking water, although Aggie knows the way so well, I believe she could find it in the dark. What am I saying? Everything and every time is dark for my brave elder sister.

When we first came here, Aggie would try to find her way around this strange new place, inching along, hands held out, stumbling over logs and river stones, but always picking herself up and trying again. The Maori women would touch her face gently, stroke her sightless eyes. Some of them would go into the bush, bring back leaves that they mashed up and held against her eyelids.

It was Hahona who helped most. She became Aggie's great friend, just as Haare is mine. The two small girls, as they were then, playing with Aggie's doll or long strips of flax, making webs and lines with their flashing fingers, chanting in English and Maori. Aggie speaks the Maori tongue well. I am moderate only; Haare's English is far better than my efforts in his language.

Around her neck, Hahona wears a piece of glowing green jade. It is a fine thing, carved like a tiny flying bat with wings outspread. Her auntie (I think she means that) gave it to her before her people moved to live beside the river, just as Auntie Flora gave Aggie her bracelet. Many times I have seen my sister holding the little greenstone carving, feeling its shape with her fingers, while Hahona tries the silver bracelet on her own wrist.

Yet bracelet and bat have caused anger. Not long after they became friends, before our house was even built, Hahona led Aggie back to our hut one night, pressed her forehead gently against my sister's, then left. As we sat down to our smoked eel and kumara —

Aggie had to be guided into her chair in those days —
Mother exclaimed 'Aggie, love! Your bracelet — where
is it?'

My sister smiled. 'Hahona is wearing it tonight.'
She touched her throat, and I saw the little green bat
hanging there, its polished stone glinting in the firelight.
'She has given me her pekapeka until tomorrow, to
show we are friends.' My mother said nothing.

Before we were halfway through our meal, we heard
an angry voice calling from outside, growing nearer
and louder. Hahona's mother, Areta, barged through
the doorway of our hut, pulling a weeping Hahona and
Ngaio behind her.

Areta is only small, but that night she seemed to fill
the room. Her eyes flashed; the blue tattoo marks on
her chin and lips gleamed. A torrent of Maori words
burst from her.

Father was splendid. He didn't understand what
Areta was shouting — none of us did. But he stood,
nodded quietly to the angry visitor, pulled out a chair,
and beckoned to her. Areta went silent, strode forward
like — like a warrior — and sat. Ngaio had scuttled
across the room to crouch beside Janet, and the two
young girls watched with staring eyes.

With signs, and Hahona's English words and Aggie's
Maori words, we slowly understood. The greenstone
bat, the pekapeka, is a great treasure. It keeps away
evil, and gives strength to the person who wears it. If

it were taken, that person and the whole tribe would grow weak and suffer.

'Areta says they have lost other treasures,' Aggie explained. 'Some from fighting, some hidden in the — the water? The—?' My sister turned to Hahona who had stopped crying, and stood clutching the silver bracelet in her hand. 'Swamp' went the Maori girl.

'Swammup,' repeated her mother, nodding until her glossy black hair bobbed.

'That mucky old bit o' land?' My father stroked his beard. 'I was planning tae drain that tae make new grazing for our cows. Would your folks mind, Hahona?'

It took more time to explain all this. Areta sat watching us, upright on her chair. When she understood, her eyes blazed again, and more Maori words poured out.

'The swamp holds secrets,' Aggie said, after she and Hahona had talked together still more, and I stood uselessly by. 'Dear things are there. Treasures. Areta says it is . . . I think she means holy.'

I thought of that muddy bog with its flax and birds, and nearly laughed out loud. Father shook his head once at me, and I stopped. Mother was placing a mug of tea in Areta's hands. Our fiery visitor bent her head, sniffed, sipped, exclaimed 'Kah-pai!'

My father nodded to Hahona. 'Will ye tell your mother that we will never touch the swamp. We know what holy land is; we have had tae leave ours far behind. Och, and tell her that you and Maggie wore each other's treasures because you are like sisters.'

I saw the tears in my blind sister's eyes, and felt shame at almost having laughed. Aggie leaned her fair head against Hahona's dark one, and the two of them murmured together once more. They spoke to Areta, and as they did so the tattooed chin came up, and the Maori woman stood. She gazed at my father. Her head only reached his chest, but they were like two leaders facing each other. She took one of Father's huge hands in both hers, pressed it to her heart for a moment. I couldn't understand the words she spoke, but I could guess what they meant. My mother watched, smiling.

Father shook his head in an embarrassed kind of manner. 'Och, it's no' a bother. It'll make up for that time with the bagpipes.'

Now Aggie and Mother and I and little Janet did burst out laughing. Areta and her daughters looked startled, so I tucked an imaginary pair of pipes under my arm, and pretended to blow. 'Whaaa-ooo!' I went. Areta shrieked, and clamped her hands over her ears. Then she, Hahona and Ngaio were laughing, too.

A few years after we reached New Zealand, another steamship with families from the Highlands arrived.

Mother's cousin Hamish stayed with us for the winter, before travelling on to look for land. He had brought his bagpipes all the way from Scotland. I was just a lad of eight or nine then, but I remember the first fine morning Hamish was with us, when he stepped outside our hut into the clear, cold air, drew a deep breath, and began to play.

'A Song of the Morning', the tune was called. But the Maori people who were cooking breakfast or fetching water from the river didn't sing. At the first 'Whaaa-ooo!', children screamed, and ran for their parents. I saw Hahona staring with her mouth open, Ngaio's terrified face, Haare springing forward to protect his sisters.

'Whaaa-oooo!' Men rushed out with spears or stone clubs, and stood in front of their families. Magpies and other birds exploded squawking from the trees.

Hamish saw what was happening, took the pipes from his mouth, and the sound died away. For a few seconds, nobody moved or spoke. Then Father began laughing. Some of the Maori men joined in, and soon everyone except a few scared babies was giggling and shouting. Haare and I rushed around, calling 'Whaaaa-oooo!'

Areta and her people wanted to touch the pipes, but when the bag made a sighing sound, they jumped back, then laughed again. Ngaio clung to her mother and wouldn't look, until Janet took her hand and placed it on the chanter pipe.

After that, Hamish began to play — very softly — another tune, a lament at leaving home. Father put a big arm around Mother, and they stood together until Hamish had finished. She dabbed her eyes; Maori women murmured and nodded.

'That is your taonga?' one asked. 'Your treasure?'

'Aye, it is that,' Father said, and they nodded again.

That treasure left with Mother's cousin, but people here still talk about it. The Crying Tah-nee-wha — monster — they call it.

A few nights after we talked about it being nearly eleven years since we arrived, more people stood in the doorway of our house. Haare, Ngaio, Hahona, and the young man who will be the father of her child. 'Greetings, friends.' Haare nodded to us all. 'John Brady comes tomorrow to take flax to town. Are there other things he should carry? Do people wish to travel with him?'

Hahona whispered something to Aggie, and my big sister blushed. My parents smiled at each other. 'Aggie, dear,' Mother said, 'I'm thinking we need some flour and salt from town. Would ye mind too much riding in with John tomorrow?' My sister blushed again, while Hahona tried to hide her smiles.

Then Aggie's friend looked across the room to where I sat, turned, and spoke to Ngaio, who had gone to sit as usual beside Janet. The girl glanced at me; hung her head. My face felt hot. Dear Lord, surely I wasn't blushing, too?

★

It was long before I slept. I lay under my blankets listening to the little owls, the ru-ru, call from the forest. I thought of that night years ago, when Ngaio was but young, dragged to our hut with Hahona by her angry mother. Now she is growing into a woman. I have already said it, but tonight I suddenly saw it as well.

When I burned with fever on the *Princess Louisa*, Aggie would murmur stories to me of the bright new life waiting for us in faraway New Zealand, and the riches we might find there. It was hard to believe in anything bright, after my poor sister lost her sight. But now I remembered Areta's talk of the secret things that may lie in the swamp. I smiled as I thought how Mother would call each of us 'm'wee treasure' when we were small. Indeed, I suppose people can be treasures, too. Ngaio . . . I shook my head at myself.

At school, Mr McDougall told us of gold and silver buried in the graves of ancient kings, or precious weapons found on battlefields of long ago. In our holidays, when we did not have to work, Haare and I sometimes explored beside the Why-Mow-Ana River, or under the trees of the bush, hoping to find such things.

Heaven knows, there are enough battlefields in this country where tribe fought against tribe or settler against Maori. Bitter places, all of them. But no gold or jewels did we ever find.

It makes me laugh to think of such things now. We have been so busy clearing the bush, building our homes, making roads, that we have little time to think of treasure. But when I get my horse (there is a fine young black colt belonging to Mr Sheffield up the valley; his name is Chieftain), I will explore all over this land, and who knows what I may find?

Sometimes I dream of a different sort of riches: those of travelling, of seeing strange countries. There is talk of a second war with the Dutch rebels in South Africa. They fought against Britain some years ago; now trouble is brewing again. Lads with whom I went to school say they want to join the Army if war does come again, to fight against these Boers. It will be a great adventure.

Yet Father needs me here. He is strong and fit, but the first grey is in his hair and beard.

And now there is this other thing. When Hahona spoke to Ngaio tonight, and the young girl glanced at me, I felt my heart move inside me. What can it all mean?

In the morning, I set off along the riverbank, searching for one of our cows. Strawberry (named after her red coat) keeps wandering away.

Women from the pa were at the water's edge, checking the nets and traps they set to catch eels, and the little inanga fish that taste so good when we cook them with flour. We greeted one another. I found myself looking to see if Ngaio was among them, but she was not there.

Here is another memory: they all seem to be coming just now.

One summer night, when Haare and I were about . . . eleven? twelve? . . . he and I took fishing lines and went to the shelves of rock reaching out into the river. Janet and Ngaio pestered us until we finally let them come, too.

The world was quiet and still. Stars glittered across the sky. Haare showed me the great canoe that Maori people see in the heavens: the three stars of its prow, the little group that make its stern, the long line like rope, twisting across the sky to the four-starred anchor we call the Southern Cross. Mother has talked of the different stars that shine above Scotland. Perhaps I will see them sometime.

That night, we fixed pieces of meat on our hooks, and Haare broke a rotten egg into the water, since eels are said to like that smell. Janet and Ngaio held their noses. Then we sat on the rocks and talked softly.

Something snatched at my line. It was so strong, so sudden, that I almost toppled into the river. Haare seized me, and we began hauling in, hand over hand. In the water, a black shape struggled and writhed. Three more heaves, and it was thrashing on the rocks among the four of us. An eel as long as my arms: dinner for our whole family.

I tried to stamp on it, while Haare struck at it with a stone. The two girls ran and leaped in circles, screaming. Haare turned his head to shout at them; the stone in his hand missed the eel and hit my bare foot. Our dinner jerked itself off the hook, and twisted back into the water.

I was hopping on one foot, Ngaio and Janet were still jumping and shrieking, and my friend was bent over, laughing so much he almost burst. We teased the girls for weeks afterwards about their screaming. Now I don't know if I can tease Ngaio any more.

This morning, I saw Strawberry where she was munching on shrubs (not the deadly tutu; cows seem to know) at the edge of the bush. She gazed at me with her huge brown eyes, and swished her tail. I glanced around to make sure nobody could see me, then I put my arms around her neck, and leaned my head against her, while she breathed warm, leaf-smelling air on me.

We plodded back downriver towards our farm. Blue smoke curled from the chimney, where Mother and Aggie would be cooking breakfast. My blind sister is as skilful in the kitchen as anyone. Janet crossed the yard towards the milking bail, carrying a bucket in each hand. When did she grow so tall?

Fences gleamed in the morning sun. Our two fields — paddocks, we call them here — still have old tree stumps, but grass grows thick and soft. As I came up, with Strawberry moving slow and gentle ahead of me, I could truly believe that this was a land where riches might be found. I smiled at myself. You're a man now, I thought. You shouldn't be thinking of childish things like this.

The Why-Mow-Ana slid past in its rocky bed. A pair of ducks fussed at the edge. Haare and I hunted them with wooden spears when we were ten or twelve, but the only time we hit one, we got such a shock that we stood and stared. The spear took away half the bird's tail feathers; it rose with a furious *qu-aaawwkk!* and flew off towards the swamp, fast — and crooked.

Whole families of ducks live in the swamp; they seem to know they're safe there.

Our river is always changing. I have mentioned how it becomes a thundering torrent after days of rain, impossible to cross. Twice while we have lived here, floodwaters have carved a new path, gouging their way through the sand and shingle, sometimes ripping away the roots of trees so they topple into the current. Our favourite swimming and fishing place, the one by the rocks, became a shallow pool last year, then was a deep bend again, just six months later.

Strawberry paced into the paddock. I tied her to the milking bail with a rope around her neck (I hardly need it; she's such a gentle beast), and sat down on the stump that is our milking stool. My hands went to work, and warm streams of milk began hissing into the pail.

'Niall!' Aggie called after a while. 'Breakfast!'

At the same time, I heard a bumping of wheels, and saw John Brady's wagon jolting up the track towards our house. Its tray was stacked with bundles of flax that John takes to the nearest railway. Two figures sat among the bundles: Hahona and her young man.

My elder sister walked across to meet them. You would never guess she cannot see, except for the way she tests each step for half a second before she takes her next. John Brady swung down, spoke to her so she knew where he was, held out his hand. My sister took it.

He is indeed a good man. I hope a life lies ahead for him and Aggie.

Seeing her and Hahona made me think again of Ngaio. How strange to look at someone you have known for a long time, and suddenly see a different person. I shook my head. Time will tell.

I stood and untied Strawberry. The smell of fresh bread drifted from the house. Aggie, John and Hahona were laughing, while Hahona's young man stood by, shy but proud. Magpies warbled from the bush; the world glittered in early morning sunlight.

I gazed around me, then lifted the brimming pail and set off towards the others. Someday I may search for those other treasures, I told myself. In the meantime, this will satisfy me.

DUNCAN

1918

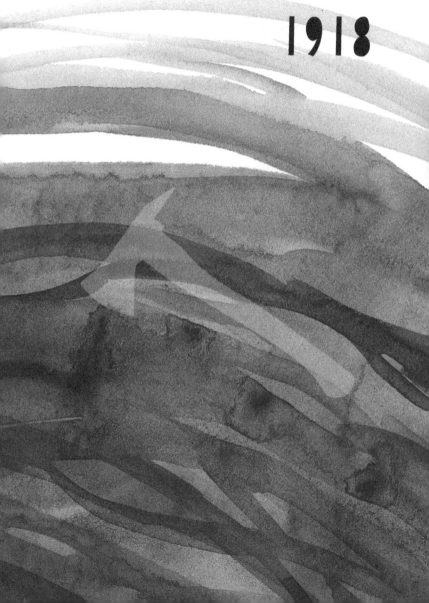

My mother looked at me and smiled as I set out this morning. She does look, even though she can't see me. Her eyes are blind, yet they seem to gaze into people. She lost her sight when she caught scarlet fever on the voyage from Scotland to New Zealand. (They came in a ship which had sails; can you imagine that?) She was just a girl then, and she learned to do everything without her sight: cook, sew, make her garden. My father, John, says she can somehow feel the colours in flowers with her fingers. She plants them always in perfect patterns.

Mother smiled at me even though I was in such a black mood. I had argued with my father last night. 'You don't need to go, Duncan, lad,' he said. 'The war will end soon; the Germans are on the run. There's no need to be rash. Your mother would—' He stopped himself.

I knew what he meant, even though Mother has never spoken to me about how she feels. But I heard my voice rising. 'Other blokes from around here have gone. I don't want to be a coward!'

We got louder. My young sister, Jess, sat and said nothing. It's a rare thing for Jess to be silent; she and her friend Lily Sheffield have all sorts of strange ideas — learning to speak Maori, or women being in Parliament — and usually she's all too ready to tell the world what she thinks. But last night, she stayed quiet.

Father and I were polite to each other at breakfast. He drove off in the truck, sitting straight like he always does, as if he were riding a horse. You see fewer horses in our district now. Thousands of the poor creatures have been shipped overseas to pull guns and wagons in the terrible battles of the Western Front. And a truck can do the work of six horses. I told Father so one time; said we had to look to the future. 'A horse doesn't get punctures, Duncan,' he went. 'It doesn't run out of petrol.' And then — then he went out and bought a truck to carry his flax and other goods.

I crossed our home paddock, past the macrocarpas planted to give us firewood someday. I half-slid down the bank, then sloshed my way across the Waimoana, using the axe to hold me steady against the current. The water was only up to my thighs; it's been a dry summer. Trout were brought from Scotland and released into our rivers years ago; Father and Uncle Niall and I enjoy catching them. They'd mostly be in the cool, deep pools just now.

Our river isn't always easy to cross. Just two years ago, Father and I had to ford it after heavy rain. He wanted to visit his and Uncle Niall's friend Haare, who lives in the pa on the other side. Haare was ill; he gets sick a lot in winter, and Father was determined to see him.

He didn't tell Mother we were going; she'd have tried to stop him. But when we reached the new paddock he'd cleared beside the river, he said, 'Come with me, Duncan, lad. We can manage this.' So we climbed down to where the Waimoana was wider and didn't seem so deep. Father carried a long stick. 'We'll hold this, Duncan. Four legs will stand against the current better than two. We could do with one of your uncle's horses.'

Uncle Niall is a wonderful rider. There's a story I used to make Mother or Father tell me over and over about his first horse, big black Chieftain, and what happened when my uncle set off to fight in the South African war.

On the morning I'm talking about, Father and I waded into the current. The water surged around us, knee-deep, then hip-deep, then waist-deep. The river ran brown and noisy; we couldn't see its bed, but I heard rocks rumbling along it. The stick held us steady; one of us stood still while the other took a step, and we laboured forward.

We were over halfway to the far side. Father reached a foot forward, staggered, then plunged down. He'd stepped into a hole in the riverbed.

His hand slipped from the stick. I saw the water begin to tear him away. My free hand shot forward, I grasped his collar and hung on with all my strength. My other hand rammed the stick into the bed of the river, bracing us. Father hauled himself upright, grunting and spluttering. He seized his end of the stick once more, and we waded on.

Neither of us spoke until we reached the far bank and crouched panting on the ground, dragging breath back into our bodies. Then Father placed a hand on my shoulder. 'You'll be a fine, strong man, Duncan.' That was all he said, but it warmed me then, and it still warms me now when I think about it. And it makes me sad that there is this difference between us.

What am I to do? I do not believe that war is right. Men should not kill one another just because their governments tell them to. Because I work on a farm, I can probably be excused from the Army; New Zealand farms are vital in producing the meat and cheese to feed Britain. But should I stay safe at home when so many young men I know are putting their lives at risk?

After I crossed the river this morning, I lifted the axe onto my shoulder and set off towards where our orchard will be planted. The rocks of our swimming hole glowed in the early sun. A bridge will be built near there some day — but not until the war is over, so money and men are here to start it.

The ground I'd cleared over the past three weeks lay ahead. I felt proud at how much I'd done, yet sorry that the tall totara and kahikatea (Uncle Niall knows all their names; Haare taught him) have to fall. Plums, apples and pears will stand in their place. Mother already imagines herself and Jess bottling the fruit. 'Why just us?' my sister wanted to know. 'Why can't men learn to do such things, also?' Those are the sorts of strange ideas she comes out with.

I reached the kahikatea I was going to fell first today, leaned my axe against its trunk, and took off my coat. But instead of beginning the cut, I stood gazing into the cool bush. Arthur Smale, from two miles up the valley, left to start his army training last week. He's just the latest from our district. His brother, George, has been fighting in France for two years now; he wrote home that he'd met Scottish soldiers who came from the Highlands where Mother's family used to live. Mother was silent for a whole day when she heard.

And here was I, still trying to decide whether to enlist. I knew how Mother felt; she said it nearly broke Mrs Smale's heart when both her sons joined up. But . . . I sighed as I stood and stared around.

The war has been raging for nearly four years now, and everybody says the Germans and their allies are being pushed back everywhere. Our forces have won huge areas of land back from Turkey; Italy has defeated the Kaiser's Austro-Hungarian supporters; Germany itself is running out of men and supplies. 'We've got the Hun on the run!' people sing at fund-raising concerts.

Millions of men — and women and children — have died. My father and Uncle Niall shake their heads when they talk of it. What shall I do? Killing is wrong, yet I have a duty to my country and the British Empire.

The air had begun to shimmer above the swamp that lies beyond our swimming rocks. Mr Sheffield, who owns the biggest farm in the valley, would like to see the swamp drained. 'Good land going to waste, John,' I heard him tell my father once. But it's a special place to Maori people; they have stories of treasure hidden there.

'Stuff and nonsense!' grunted Mr Sheffield, when Father reminded him of this. He was in a bad mood, because Mother and Uncle Niall had told him we'd already taken too much from the Maori, and it was time we left them what was rightfully theirs.

'There's *real* riches, good money in this land, if we develop it properly,' Mr Sheffield snapped. My parents and Uncle Niall nodded politely, but stood firm.

A hawk hovered above the swamp. There always

seems to be one there — just one, never any more. Magpies scolded it from trees nearby. Mother told me once of a hawk she'd seen in Scotland, just before their ship sailed and when she could still see. 'It shone like a jewel, Duncan lad,' she murmured, and I seemed to see it myself, hanging like this one in the morning sky.

Treasure . . . jewels: I had work to do! I spat on my palms, seized the axe, and made the first cut.

I'm good with an axe. Father says so. He taught me how to let its heavy steel head do the work, to keep my footing secure, legs wide apart, shoulders swinging loosely, angling the blade so it cuts a deep V, then widens it, never sticking or jamming. I began to relax as the blade lifted, fell, bit. The notch deepened. Sweet-smelling chips flew; my body grew warmer.

Mr Sheffield says every young man must fight for King and Country. He and his daughter Lily argue about it, Jess says. She and Lily are the same age, fast friends with the same strange views about what women can do.

Lily is a tall lass, with dark hair and green eyes. Those eyes look hard at me when she asks me questions — and she's always asking, like Jess. Just because men are stronger than women, does that make them better? Does any government have the right to force a mother's son to fight? I didn't like her at first: the spoiled daughter of a rich landowner, I thought. Aunt Janet married into a family like the Sheffields, and now she lives at the other end of the country. She told Mother she couldn't understand why people wanted to spend their lives grubbing around in a backward place like this. We get just one letter a year from her, at Christmas.

So yes, I felt suspicious of Lily at first. She thinks she's cleverer than I am, I grumbled to myself. But now, I look forward to her company, her lively mind and green eyes. At times, I have even thought . . .

Work! The axe thudded home. The kahikatea's trunk began to tremble. I lifted and struck; lifted and struck again. A creaking, groaning noise grew. I stepped back quickly as the tree leaned, paused, then fell with a tearing crash, branches thrashing at other trees as it toppled. The trunk bounced, then lay still. Dust rose; magpies swore at me. There would be a month's firewood in that trunk. I felt pleased at what I'd done, yet sad at the sight of the tall shape, lifeless on the ground.

I sat and drank from the bottle of now lukewarm tea Mother had made for me. The land our orchard will grow on once belonged to the Maori people. Father bought it from them. He and Uncle Niall and their friend Haare — who was well then — cut down the first tree from the bush together, and sawed it into planks that made a new bedroom for our farmhouse. Mother and Uncle Niall and Aunt Janet spent their first years in New Zealand living in a one-roomed hut where our house now stands. And now the house has changed so much, Mother says Grandma and Grandfather would never recognise it.

Grandfather Angus died when I was about ten, and Grandma Helen three years later. They're buried in the cemetery above the river. I remember the Maori women sitting beside their coffins and wailing. Mother says we'd never have survived in this land if it hadn't been for the kindness of her friend Hahona's tribe during the first winters. When the old lady Areta died, Mother wept at her graveside.

Jess says we should all learn the Maori language, because it's starting to fade away. We expect Maori people to learn English, yet we can't be bothered knowing their words. Uncle Niall agrees. It's another thing I can't make up my mind about.

I picked up my axe, ran the sharpening stone back and forth over its edge. Father says you must keep your axe so sharp you can shave with it. I haven't tried that!

The next tree was a totara, tough and knotty. There'd be a few hours' work in this one. I spat on my hands again, scraped a mark on the trunk, and swung. The blade bit and stuck. I wrenched at it, and it came away with a squealing sound.

Suddenly I had another memory of Grandfather Angus's funeral. One of Grandmother's cousins, called Hamish, rode for two days from his home, in order to play the bagpipes at the burial. As the first notes wailed across the crowd of mourners, children pressed their hands over their ears or cried. Maori people stared, except for Hahona and Haare and my Aunt Ngaio, who began smiling and whispering to one another for some reason.

I swung, tugged at the blade, swung again. Hard work. I didn't care. It helped take my mind off the choice I had to make. Did I fight, and possibly kill? Or did I refuse, and seem a coward? Uncle Niall said that as long as I did what I believed in, I could be proud. But how did I know what I believed?

Uncle Niall chose to fight — in the South African war, the Boer War, against Dutch rebels. Grandmother and Grandfather didn't want him to join up.

'We've little tae thank the English for,' Grandfather Angus said. 'They drove many of us from our land.' But Niall went, because his friends were enlisting — and because it was going to be a great adventure, he told me once. He came back with a smashed shoulder from a Boer bullet, which means he can't work on a farm any longer. That's why he and Aunt Ngaio run the flax mill just outside town.

He came back to his own horse, too. I haven't yet told you the famous story about Chieftain. Too many other problems to think about . . .

★

I'd started cutting the totara in one of its knottiest parts. I hadn't examined it properly; how foolish. But I had to keep going now. I chopped, heaved at the axe until it came free, heard myself grunt. Usually, the rhythm of work helped me think. This blasted tree was *stopping* me from thinking! I just couldn't make up my mind.

I paused to take deep breaths. Something moved upriver. A man crossing on a horse. Rawiri, Hahona's son. He'd offered to help me clear the bush for our orchard, but his mother wouldn't let him. Ever since her husband was killed by a falling tree while he worked in the next valley, Hahona has believed the bush is taking revenge on Maori people who sold their land.

Rawiri's family have always been friends with ours. Hahona and Mother got into trouble when they were young because Hahona lent Mother her pekapeka, the carved greenstone bat she wears around her neck. It was like letting a sacred treasure pass out of her care, and her mother, Areta, came storming over to our place to get it back. The girls meant no harm; Mother had lent Hahona her silver bracelet from Scotland, with its thistle clasp. That's one of *our* treasures, I suppose. Lily Sheffield has a silver bracelet, too; I wager hers cost more.

Hahona and Rawiri live with Uncle Niall and Aunt Ngaio now. My aunt and uncle have no children of their own. Their mill is not far from the school (a bigger school these days), and Auntie Ngaio used to stand watching the children as they passed by each morning. So my clever mother talked to Mr McDougall, the headmaster, and he invited my aunt to come and teach the classes some Maori songs and games. She's been doing it ever since, and Uncle Niall says it's like having fifty children!

He's a fine teacher, is Mr McDougall. He came in my last year at school, just before I turned fourteen, and he still lends me books. Mother and Father exclaimed when they heard his name. His uncle was the first headmaster, and lies in our cemetery, just across from Hahona's husband and not far from my grandparents. People are often near to one another in our little district, sometimes in sad ways.

Maybe I can talk to Mr McDougall about whether I should join the Army, I thought, all of a sudden. I had to do something to make up my mind.

The axe blade stuck again. I pulled at it, but it wouldn't come out. I twisted the handle, braced my foot against the totara, and heaved. The steel head jerked free, and I staggered backwards. I could hear myself panting. Don't hurry when you're chopping, Father always says.

A calm mind makes a clean cut. But I didn't seem able to stay calm today.

I wiped sweat from my forehead. Voices rose from the far side of the river. Jess and . . . Mother, was it? No, Lily. That's right; they were going to move all the cows from one paddock to another for Father. That's another thing Jess says: that it's nonsense to talk of some work being 'not ladylike'. Women should be allowed to do any job they're capable of.

She and Lily are reading books on nursing just now. 'If this dreadful war keeps on, we want to help in some way,' Lily told me last week. I don't know what rich Mr Sheffield would think about his daughter being mixed up with blood and sickness.

I snorted suddenly, as I tried to imagine what he'd think about his daughter helping shoo cows out of a paddock. He's had one of those new milking machines installed on his farm. 'Does the work in half the time, John!' he told my father. 'And only needs half as many workers!' But Father told Mother at dinner that he *likes* milking our cows by hand — their warm grassy smell, their soft coats, the silence as he works. And he wondered what the workers whom Mr Sheffield had replaced with his new machine would do to earn a living now.

Once more the axe wedged in the knotty wood. I'd never get the tree felled at this rate. I'd never get my mind made up either, it seemed. Enlist and kill? Stay and be shamed? It was hopeless.

I wrenched and twisted. I seized a rock, and beat on the axe head where it was stuck in the trunk. If Father saw me, he'd be horrified. Finally, the axe came away. A thick knot showed, right where I was cutting. It would take me an hour just to get through that. I stood, gripping the axe. Sweat dripped into my eyes.

Suddenly I felt so angry. Angry at having to choose between war and shame; at how other people didn't seem to have such problems; at the stupid tree for being full of knots; the axe for jamming. At everything.

I took a stride forward. I drew the axe back, yelled 'Choose!', and swung it at the totara, putting all my weight behind it.

Beneath my foot, a wood-chip or something rolled sideways. I lurched as the heavy steel blade flashed down at the wood. It hit the knot, skidded off, and sliced into my left leg, just above the knee.

I felt no pain. But I heard the noise it made: a *chock* like Mother's meat cleaver slicing into the roast as she prepares dinner. And then a different sound, as the axe head struck something harder, deep inside my flesh. My leg collapsed under me, and I fell.

There was still no pain, only a feeling of strangeness. But I knew straightaway. I'd done something terrible, something that would change me forever. I sprawled half on my side, among the wood-chips and trampled earth of my chopping. I lifted myself on one elbow, and made myself look.

The axe lay beside my body. Something wet gleamed on its blade. My left leg was stretched out; it looked just ordinary. My trousers had a small rip in them, halfway down. Mother will be vexed at me for making more mending, I thought foolishly.

The leg felt hot, and distant somehow. I dragged in breaths, pulled myself over the ground on my elbows to the totara, wrenched my body around so that I sat with my back to the trunk. I heard myself making grunting, gasping sounds. A terrible fear had begun rising in me.

My left trouser leg was changing colour, even as I watched. A red wetness spread across it, glistening in the sunlight. The whole leg felt weak now; it seemed to only half-belong to me. I sat, mouth open, still gasping. Then I clenched my teeth together and pulled up my trouser leg. It came easily, slipping sodden and heavy over my knee. I closed my eyes for a second, then forced them open and stared down.

The flesh sagged away from a hand-sized trench above my knee. Blood gushed from it, pouring over my thigh, soaking into cloth and ground. Deep inside the wound, something showed white for a second, before another flood of blood covered it.

The pain hit. It exploded through me, a tearing and clawing that jerked my head back against the tree, and sent howls echoing into the bright air. Magpies nearby shrieked in return. I clamped both hands over the ripped flesh, wailing and shuddering.

My teeth ground together so hard I thought they would splinter. My heart hammered. Terror pulsed through me. I was going to die.

With no warning, the terror vanished, and I was angry again. Not just angry: wild with fury. I'd used the axe like a maniac; broken every rule my father had taught me. I'd die here, and I had nobody to blame except myself.

My hands moved. They tore at the buttons of my shirt, dragging it from my back. They stopped as I hunched in another surge of agony, screamed again. Then they were wrapping the shirt around the gaping wound, pulling it tight, then tighter still while I sobbed and whimpered, tugging at the sleeves with every bit of strength I had, knotting them over and over. Instantly, the cloth began turning sodden red.

Above the noises I was making, part of my mind kept working. I had to get home. Mother and Jess were there. And Lily. I had to cross the river before I lost too much blood. I couldn't. I must.

I clutched the totara's rough bark and started hauling myself up. My left leg flopped. I forced myself to put weight on it, shrieked and half-fell, holding onto the tree-trunk. I couldn't walk. My leg was useless. I had no chance.

The axe lay nearby. I groped for it, rammed the head into the ground beside me, and levered myself up again, hunched over it. Sweat streamed from me; my face twisted with the pain. Somebody was moaning 'Aaah! Help! Help!' My own voice, yet it seemed to come from miles away.

I held my breath. I'd use the axe like a stick, get across the river and up the bank with it. I took a step forward and screamed again. Pain jolted my whole left side. I *heard* my body shudder with it. I lifted my head, teeth grinding together. I fixed my eyes on the Waimoana, thirty yards away, and began to move.

The shirt tied around my leg meant I could walk only by swinging the leg forward, then dragging it after me. Every time it touched the ground, I cried aloud with agony. Sweat poured down my naked upper body. I forced myself on, step by step.

Ten . . . twelve paces, and I was out into the full sunlight. My foot squelched inside the boot; my left trouser leg sagged, sodden with blood. I stared around as I hobbled on. Would Rawiri reappear? But there was only the hawk upriver, gliding above the swamp. Nobody would expect to see me until evening. I was going to die alone.

Thump went the axe head on the ground. *Thump*. I stumbled forwards, my ruined leg dragging and jarring at each step. I squeezed my eyes shut, blundered towards the water.

Chink! A different sound. 'Aaahh!' I howled again as the shock of the axe head hitting rock beat through me. I stared down, and I was onto the stones of the riverbed.

One step. Then another. I couldn't stop. If I did, I might never be able to start again. I was losing blood all the time. I could see it dripping through the shirt, feel it sliding down into my boot. I took another step, and red drops sprinkled the rocks around. How long before I fainted, or was so weak, I couldn't keep going?

The river was just ahead, sparkling along. How could I wade it and get up the bank? Screaming was no use. Jess and Lily would have gone back inside by now. If only we had a bridge. If only this damned war hadn't taken men away, there would be a bridge, with trucks and wagons passing to help me. It was the war's fault!

No, it wasn't. I understood that again as I reeled over the stones. It was my own stupid temper, my being unable to choose. I had put myself in this plight, and only I could get myself out. I lifted my head again, shouted 'Come on!' Two ducks rose honking from the shallows nearby, and flapped off.

I floundered into the Waimoana. The water chilled my shuddering body. I stepped on an unseen rock, shrieked again as my left leg buckled sideways. Clouds of blood drifted away in the current.

My head was down, searching for any holes in the riverbed. If I fell, as Father had that time, I was done for. My strength was beginning to ebb. The pain surged through me with every lurching step. I was up to my knees; I must be halfway there. My voice still sobbed, but it felt further and further away. The bright day was growing dark at the edges. God, I'd never make it. Climbing the bank was impossible.

I had no choice. The words stood in my mind so clearly, it was as if I'd read them from Mr McDougall's blackboard. If I didn't get up the bank, I was dead. Even if I did get up . . . but I couldn't think about that. Just fifteen minutes ago I'd been fretting over a different choice. It seemed so unimportant now.

Something thudded into my bare chest. I cried out, staggered and almost fell. It was the far bank; I'd got across the river. I gripped a shrub with my free hand; kept the axe braced on the riverbed. Breath rasped in my lungs. My body wouldn't stop trembling. I stared up at the steep slope of tree roots and shrubs. It looked enormous; I couldn't climb it.

My head jerked, staring upriver, then down. No sign of anybody. I was alone. I began sagging down into the water. I couldn't climb the bank. I'd die here like a . . .

Like a coward. The word almost rang in my head.

Next second, I was throwing myself upwards, out of the water, snatching at roots and shrubs with one hand. My other arm swung the axe as if it was a toy, driving its metal head into the bank, hauling myself upwards, foot by foot.

My maimed leg sent pain hammering through me. I howled like an animal, screamed with every clutch and move. I heard my shrieks echoing all around. Grab. Haul. Swing. Grab. Haul. Swing. The agony grew.

Darkness started to spread in front of my eyes. I didn't even know if I was still moving.

I swung the axe once more. It met emptiness, flew forward out of my hand. The top half of my body collapsed across flat ground. I screamed again at the shock. I'd reached the top of the bank.

Other voices shouted. Somehow, I lifted my head. Jess and Lily were rushing towards me, eyes staring, skirts flying. Lily's dark hair streamed behind her. Mother was struggling across the paddock as well, yards further back, hands out in front of her.

'Duncan!' my sister gasped. 'What's wrong? What happened?' The two of them reached me where I sprawled on the ground, sodden, shaking, bleeding.

'My leg,' I grunted. 'Axe—'

Lily saw. She dropped to her knees beside me, pressed her hands hard over my knotted, blood-soaked shirt. 'Take his belt off, Jess! We'll tie it around his thigh — make a tourniquet!'

My sister threw herself down, too. Her face was pale. She bit her lip. Next second, she'd unbuckled my belt, dragged it out of the trouser loops, and was pulling it around my leg, above the wound. The two young women dragged on it together; I felt the leather bite into my flesh.

Mother had arrived. She stood, hands pressed to her face, as Jess gasped out what had happened. She whipped the shawl from her shoulders, crouched beside me, began knotting the shawl around the sodden shirt.

'John will be back any minute,' she told the girls. 'One of you run and tell him! We'll get Duncan straight to town and the doctor.' Jess stood, began hurrying away. 'Bring some sheets!' Mother called. 'We'll tear them up, use them for bandages.'

'There's less blood now,' Lily murmured. 'The tourniquet must be working.' Her white face was only a few inches from mine; her bottom lip trembled. But she managed a shaky half-smile. 'Just as well Jess and I have been reading those nursing books.'

I tried to speak, but my voice wouldn't come. The pain had sunk to a slow, pulsing jolt. My drenched clothes felt strangely comfortable. Mother was clasping my hand, whispering 'You'll be all right, son. You'll be all right.' Lily kept pressing on the wad of clothes over my gashed flesh.

Yes, I *was* going to be all right. Somehow, I knew it. And the funny thing was, I wouldn't need to make a choice after all. The axe had made it for me.

More magpies fluted somewhere. I was drifting into darkness. My eyelids felt heavy. But I kept watching Lily Sheffield's face. The dark eyes; the lips set firm now; the neat chin. She glanced at me; tried to smile once more.

That's interesting, I thought, as the world faded. I *have* made a choice. A totally different one. And . . . And I think I've found a treasure.

FLORENCE
1938

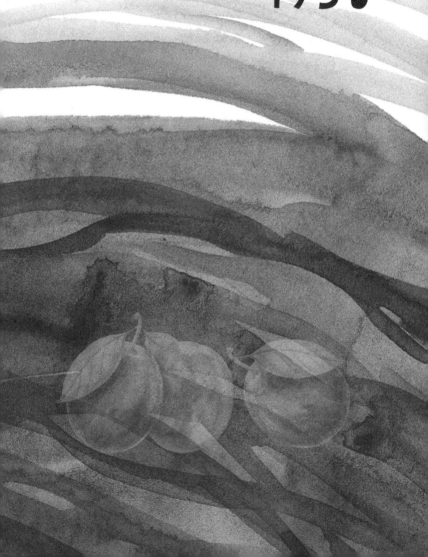

When I asked my parents why they gave the first names Florence Hahona, my father Duncan joked that the Florence was Florence Nightingale, the famous nurse.

Actually, he was only partly joking. Mostly I'm named after Great-great-auntie Flora in Scotland who gave Nana Aggie her silver bracelet. But Mum and Auntie Jess had been studying nursing before Father had his terrible accident with the axe, so the things they learned probably saved his life. And when Mum was expecting me, Auntie Jess told her: 'Lily, if this baby is a girl, she's going to bear the name of a strong woman. She's going to know that there's nothing women can't do if they get half a chance!' Fifteen years later, I've learned that when my auntie says something is going to happen, it usually does!

She — Auntie Jess — lives up in Auckland now. She started a group helping women who can't get work, or who are forced out of their homes because they don't have money to pay the rent. There was a big riot a while back, when hundreds of unemployed people marched up Queen Street, demanding that the government do more to help. When the police tried to stop them, fights started and shop windows got smashed.

And why is my second name Hahona? That's easy. She's my second nana; she and Nana Aggie have been friends nearly all their lives. They met just after Nana Aggie and Great-uncle Niall and their parents arrived from Scotland.

Great-uncle Niall told me not long before he died how he remembered their heads together as they talked and giggled and whispered: one dark and one fair. They're both white heads now, but they're still often together.

★

We could do with a couple more strong women right now, I thought, as Whina and I picked up the heavy wooden ladder Dad had made, and struggled over to the next plum tree. We'd already filled one sugar-bag with pears and apples. The orchard grows so much fruit, my parents give lots of it away.

'Well, the trees should grow well,' Dad said once, 'there's plenty of my blood in the ground to fertilise them.'

Mum went 'Duncan!' Then she stroked his cheek. They're still lovey-dovey at their age; it's embarrassing sometimes. But it must have been so scary when he hurt himself the way he did. He's still got the axe; uses it to chop wood for our stove. Nana Hahona and Great-aunt Ngaio wanted him to throw it away; they said that, because it had human blood on it, it would want more. But Dad told them he was going to show it who was boss. 'I've got unfinished business with this axe,' he said — whatever that means.

He always keeps it clean and sharp. Once I saw him holding it, staring at the heavy metal blade and shaking his head before he limped across to the wood-shed to put it away. He can't climb the ladder to pick fruit in the orchard any more. His leg hurts a lot of the time. But he can do most other things.

'If that bloke Hitler causes any more trouble in Europe, I'll send him a photo of me and my axe,' he told Mum as he read the paper at breakfast this morning. 'That'll scare the pants off him!'

Mr McDougall has told us about Adolf Hitler at school. He's building up a big German army. Anyone who tries to stand up to him gets sent to prison camps. 'New Zealand lost thousands of men when we fought Germany in the Great War,' I heard Nana Aggie telling Nana Hahona not long ago. 'Pray to God we never have to fight another one.'

★

There were three plum trees to pick. Grandad John and Dad left as much native bush as they could. 'Good on you,' Auntie Jess said when she was staying with us once. 'There's too many people bulldozing and burning every tree within sight, just to make money.'

'Nonsense!' Grandad Sheffield snorted. But I think he secretly admires Aunt Jess. After all, she's still his daughter's best friend.

As Whina and I approached the first plum tree, a pair of magpies squawked at us, then flapped off. Mum made me take out my hair-clips before I left home to meet Whina. If she's picking, she always takes off the silver bracelet Nana Aggie passed on to her. 'Magpies like shiny things, Florence. You don't want their beaks digging into your head because they fancy your hair-clip.'

Whina was waiting for me by Dad's Bridge. (Remind me to tell you why it's called that.) We talked about school and some of the boys who go there — nice ones and annoying ones — as we crossed. The big wire ropes that hold up the bridge curved above us; the deck creaked and swayed slightly.

The morning was already hot. A single hawk hung above the swamp. As we neared the far end of the bridge, a shiver seemed to run through the wooden boards beneath our feet. A gust of wind? No, the day was totally still.

The swamp has been there forever. Whina says there are stories about treasure hidden somewhere in it. I told her we should go and search, but we never have. It feels sort of spooky. Grandad Sheffield wanted to buy it once and turn it into farmland, but he gave up that sort of thing after Grandma Sheffield died during the big 'flu epidemic.

The 'flu must have been terrible. It was the end of 1918, and soldiers were starting to come home from the Great War, looking forward to seeing their families again. Some of them, or maybe people on other ships, had the germs, and once they got ashore, it spread through the whole country.

Over 8000 people died from it in New Zealand. Lots of Maori, especially: Whina's Grandad Haare was one of them. It wasn't like ordinary 'flu; it blocked people's lungs, attacked their whole body. If you got it really badly, you could be well on Monday morning, sick by Wednesday morning, and dead on Saturday morning.

Mum told me how a man they knew from up the valley — Arthur Smale — came back from the war without a scratch. Mr and Mrs Smale's other son had been killed just before peace came. Then Arthur caught the 'flu and died inside a week. His parents sold their farm and moved away. 'It broke their hearts,' Mum said.

He's buried up in our cemetery, not far from Grandad John and Great-uncle Niall and the others.

The 'flu nearly killed Mum, too. She and Auntie Jess were nursing sick people in the valley — this was before she and Dad got married — even though they knew how dangerous it was. She woke up one morning, burning with fever and coughing up black phlegm. When Nana Hahona heard, she and Great-aunt Ngaio came with special medicines. Nana Hahona put the little carved greenstone bat from around her neck under Mum's pillow. She slowly got better. Then a month later, Nana Sheffield became sick, and died after just four days. Mum says Grandad Sheffield nearly went mad with grief.

Doctors didn't know how to stop the 'flu. Mr McDougall told us how places were set up where people could have their throats sprayed. Sports games and films and concerts — anywhere that people might accidentally pass the 'flu on to others — were banned. Everyone was afraid; nobody knew where the sickness might strike next. There were stories of how some victims turned black, how so many people died in the worst places that they had to be buried in mass graves. None of this was true, but it made people even more frightened. Finally, the 'flu just seemed to stop by itself.

★

More magpies flapped and squawked in the plum tree as Whina and I finally got the ladder in place. One of them swooped down towards us, its big pointed beak gaping open, then veered away. 'Scram, you pakeha bird!' Whina yelled.

Mr McDougall's son, Robert, gave a morning talk at school about magpies one time. They were brought to New Zealand to get rid of pests like caterpillars and wasps. Now they've become a pest themselves. They're noisy; they kill smaller birds; they sometimes attack people who come too close to their nests.

Robert said the stories about magpies stealing shiny things aren't really true. Huh! He doesn't know everything! Father likes birds, but even he complains about magpies. Everyone's heard stories of them being shot for food during the Depression. Some people were so hungry then that they'd eat anything.

I climbed four . . . six steps up the ladder while Whina held it, and began dropping plums carefully into the sugar-bag around my waist. 'Hold it steady!' I called, as the wooden rungs shifted beneath my feet. 'I am!' Whina called back. 'You stop dancing around on it! You think you're Jean Batten or something?' We both began giggling.

Actually, I wouldn't mind being Jean Batten, all by myself up in the sky. When she made her record-breaking flight, all the way from England to New Zealand (it took over two weeks), Mum said: 'See? Women can do anything they set their minds to. You remember that, Florence!'

Our sugar-bags are old and patched, but Dad and Mum keep them to remind us of the Depression, the years when there were hardly any jobs, when some people didn't have enough to eat. Men tramped around the country, begging for work, or else were put in camps, living in tents while they dug railway tunnels or roads for the government — anything to feed their families. We were lucky, living on a farm. At least we had food.

A man came to our door one day. I was little; I don't remember it much. He was looking for work. He'd been a clerk in an office, but the firm had gone bankrupt. His wife and two small children back in Wellington were living mostly on bread and any vegetables they could grow. He still wore the suit trousers and jacket from his clerk's work, although they were thin and frayed by then.

What shocked Mum most was that, although it was pouring with rain, the only thing he had to keep himself dry was a sugar-bag, a small sack, over his head and down his back.

'A person — *any* person — in this country, having to

live like that!' I remember her telling my little brother Angus and me when we were old enough to understand. 'Your Nana Aggie and her parents came here from Scotland, believing they'd find a land of riches. Instead, it's a land where people nearly starve. Shameful!'

My father smiled at Angus and me. 'Your mother would show them a thing or two down in Parliament.' Mum began to speak again, and Dad lifted a hand. 'I know, Lily, love. It might never have happened if we had more women helping run the country. That's the truth, and you and Jess have helped me see it.' Next thing, they were giving each other a soppy hug.

Anyway, the man stayed for nearly a week. My parents found him some easy jobs to do in the garden, and gave him heaps to eat. Grandad Sheffield paid him for a day's work sorting out the office at the Sheffields' big farm ('paid him twice as much as he needed to,' said Mum, and looked proud). She found him an old oilskin coat from the hayshed, and kept his sugar-bag — it's the one I'm using now. When he left, she and Dad loaded him up with as much meat from Grandad Sheffield's place as he could carry, and some of my and Angus's clothes for his own kids. Mum said he was almost crying when he left.

★

My sugar-bag was half-full. The ladder wobbled again as I started down. 'Hold it properly!' I told Whina once more. 'I suppose you're day-dreaming about Robert McDougall?'

Whina blushed. 'I'm not! It wobbled by itself. And look at the bridge.'

I reached the ground and turned to see. The red swing-bridge was swaying slightly from side to side. We watched, but nothing else happened. 'Must have been the wind,' I said. 'And I bet you *were* thinking about Robert!'

Robert McDougall is really good at his schoolwork. So he should be, with a schoolteacher father. He may even go to university when he's older. He speaks Maori well; Great-aunt Ngaio says he's one of her star pupils.

He's sensible, too. When Whina and I and a couple of other girls asked if we could play rugby, and the rest of the boys laughed at us, Robert said 'Why not? Whina can run faster than most of you blokes!'

Whina pretended not to hear what I'd just said. She opened the sugar-bag and began checking the plums. 'There's magpie poo on some. We'd better wash them in the river.'

'Half for you, half for us,' I went. 'Mum and I will make jam.' Whina nodded. 'Us, too. Dad loves it.'

Whina's father, Rawiri, has been Dad's friend since they were kids. He brought over all sorts of plants and stuff to put on my father's leg after he nearly cut it off (eugh!). Whina's mum, Ahorangi, comes from the place where Nana Hahona's people used to live, years and years ago, so everyone was really pleased when Rawiri and Ahorangi said they were getting married.

Nana Hahona gave her the beautiful little greenstone bat to wear. When Nana Aggie heard about Ahorangi wearing it (she couldn't see it, of course, though she somehow notices almost everything), Dad says she smiled and said, 'Yes, this is the time.' Then she took off the silver bracelet that *she's* worn forever, and gave it to Mum. I think that's marvellous. I hope Whina and I will wear them some day.

We picked some more plums from the low branches of other trees, until the sugar-bag was just about full. A few more magpies told us off. We started out across the riverbed, carrying the bag between us. The stones were warm and smooth. The sun felt soft on my back.

I always felt a bit sad when I was on this part of the riverbed. Great-uncle Niall died here. He'd been going to see Nana Hahona at the pa, taking some food from him and Great-aunt Ngaio. That was before the bridge was finished, and people still had to ford the river. His horse came back a couple of hours later, without him. Mum and Dad found him lying peacefully beside the water; he'd had a heart attack.

Just about everyone from the pa and from other farms in the valley came to his funeral. The older Maori women had leaves around their heads, and they sang in voices that made my back shiver.

Great-uncle Niall's horse that day was the grand-daughter of the one he took to the South African war. The one he *meant* to take, anyway. When he joined up with the mounted rifle company — the Rough Riders — he rode his big black Chieftain all the way down to Wellington. Chieftain was put in a corral with other horses, waiting to be loaded onto a troop ship.

But the night before the ship sailed, Great-uncle Niall's horse kicked his way out of the corral and vanished into the dark. Niall had to leave without him. He spent a year fighting in South Africa on other army horses. Two of them were killed.

Chieftain? About a fortnight after the troop ship sailed, Wellington newspapers started carrying reports of a big black horse seen around the outskirts of the city. It escaped when anyone tried to capture it. A month later, the Levin paper, about 50 miles north of Wellington, reported the same horse, eating shrubs and grass from the roadside. Chieftain was trying to get home.

The months passed. Palmerston North papers, then Wanganui ones also described sightings of the black horse. It was limping now, but nobody could get near it. Then Chieftain vanished. He must have fallen over a cliff, or drowned in a river. Great-uncle Niall's family never mentioned it in their letters to him.

Then my great-uncle was wounded in the shoulder by a bullet, and sent home. Just a week after he returned to our farm, Nana Aggie and Grandad John heard him shouting and laughing outside. There he stood, his good arm around a tall, thin black horse with a lame leg, which was nuzzling its head into his chest. Chieftain had come home. Nana Aggie says the two of them were always together after that, until Chieftain died.

I stood gazing for a few seconds at the place where Great-uncle Niall had been found. Then I looked around. Everything was still. No sound, except for the Waimoana gurgling along. I glanced up at Dad's Bridge. It had stopped moving.

I usually keep an eye on the bridge if I'm down at the river. Angus likes to stand on the rails, and look over the edge. If Dad or Mum saw him, he'd get a telling-off. It's a long way down to the riverbed. Angus is spoiled, I reckon. He's five years younger than me; Dr Warburton from town had told Mum she shouldn't have any more children. Dad said she grumbled 'What would a man know about it?' Little Angus, we sometimes call him (I do it to annoy him), is named after our great-grandfather.

Anyway, Little Angus wasn't on the bridge this morning. Dad's Bridge: we call it that because my father wrote letters and nagged government people until they agreed to build it. He used to limp into their offices on his bad leg and tell them how he almost died because of having to wade the river and climb the bank. Now it's much easier for people to get around our valley.

Whina stumbled on a stone. I looked across; she was gazing up and down the riverbed. 'Bad luck,' I told her, 'Robert's not here.'

Whina didn't smile. 'Things seem . . . strange. Can you feel it?'

We stood for a few seconds. Still nothing. A couple of pukeko paced along by the river on their skinny legs. Whina shrugged. 'Too much imagining, eh?' We moved on, the sugar-bag heavy between us.

At the water's edge, we squatted down and began washing the poo-ey fruit, while the pukekos watched. A couple of Whina's plums began floating away in the current, and she had to go splashing after them. We started giggling again.

I raised my head, and blinked in the sunshine. This was so great. Being with my best friend, here by our river. Everything is so . . . so precious, I thought. I'm going to do something really exciting in my life. I'm going to do amazing things. I raised my head to tell Whina.

The riverbank gave a little shiver. The water nearby trembled. Behind us in the orchard, the magpies fell silent. The pukeko stopped moving.

Nothing else happened. After a few seconds, the pukeko stepped on. Whina stood up, slowly. Very quietly, she murmured, 'I'm scared, Florence. Something's coming.'

My heart gave a jump. I straightened up, too. The bridge was still empty; the world was warm and calm. 'What—' I began.

The pukeko took off suddenly, wings whacking the air, red legs trailing. We both jerked; I heard myself cry out.

We stared around. Everything looked ordinary. Nobody was hiding in the trees. Nothing moved on the riverbed or the bridge. Was it swaying again, just a little? I couldn't tell. Upstream, the pukeko landed, started pacing and pecking again. Stupid birds, giving us a fright like that.

Whina hadn't moved. She seemed to be listening. I couldn't hear anything. I moved a step closer to my friend. 'Shall we start heading back?'

Whina nodded. We bent to pick up the sugar-bag, where it lay on the stones. As we reached for it, the bag quivered. A tremor seemed to ripple through the air and ground. Little eddies appeared in the river beside the bank. Sand at the edges collapsed into the water.

We gaped at each other. I took another step towards Whina. Beneath my foot something shifted sideways, and I staggered. Whina reached out a hand. Then she was reeling backwards, too, as the world tore open.

A growling sound swelled upwards, deep within the ground. The whole riverbed jumped, as if a huge fist had rammed it from beneath. A thrashing, splintering noise erupted behind us, and I spun around. Whina did the same, arms stretched out as she fought to stay upright. I lurched from side to side.

The trees of the orchard tossed and flailed. Magpies exploded from them, shrieking. Leaves and twigs flew in the air. Plums rained down on the ground. We won't have to climb up to get those ones, a silly edge of my mind told me.

'Earthquake!' Whina gasped. 'Earthquake!'

Another sound came, a rattling and booming. I twisted around again and stared upriver. Dad's Bridge was bucking like a terrified animal. Its big wire cables shrieked. On the far bank, where my father had clawed his way up twenty years ago, a poplar tree ripped from the slope, dirt spraying from its roots. It smashed down into the Waimoana with a *WHOOMPFF!* that we could hear above the noise of the bridge.

Whina and I clung to each other. Her brown eyes were enormous. Another length of the river's edge slumped, and the sugar-bag of plums vanished under sand and rocks.

Whina clutched my elbows. 'We've got to get home! You come with—'

The ground punched up a second time. It dropped back, thrust up once more. We staggered in a circle, still holding each other, mouths open.

I saw the bridge twisting. Its cables screamed louder. The orchard trees kept thrashing. Branches snapped and fell; those plums would be squashed. On the far bank, another poplar went somersaulting into the water. Branches whipped backwards and forwards; trunks split open with a *CRACK!*

'Come — on!' We started struggling across the riverbed stones, towards the track leading up to the bridge. The ground shuddered and shifted. I banged against Whina; she clutched at my dress to stop me from falling.

At the top of the track, the little cottage behind the fence where a roadman lived had collapsed into splintered timber. The tall towers holding the bridge cables rocked. Dust flew from them. The cables thrummed and strained. Any second now they'd snap, and the whole bridge would plummet into the river. I had to cross it to reach home. How could I?

Whina's hand tightened on my arm. 'Look!'

Upriver, over the swamp, a haze hung in the air. It lay silvery-coloured, utterly unmoving while the rest of the world jerked and jolted. Above the mist, the hawk hovered, also motionless, wings outspread. Even as I stared, I realised how magical it looked.

'The bridge!' I panted. 'I have to get—'

'You can't!' Whina shook my arm. 'Florence, it'll fall. *You'll* fall. Come with me. Mum and Dad'll look after you. We'll get across the river a different way.'

I stared back at the Waimoana. It wasn't gurgling any longer. It stormed along, green and white fountains of water shooting upwards, bursting against the fallen poplars.

'I have to!' My voice sounded strange. 'I have to find — parents. Little Angus.'

Whina stood still. Then she placed a hand on my forehead, and murmured something in Maori. Her cotton dress was old and faded, her feet were bare, but she looked . . . powerful, somehow.

'Go, my friend. We will find each other.'

The ground had stopped shifting, but Dad's Bridge still shuddered. Voices shouted from somewhere on the other side.

I stepped onto the wooden deck; nearly jumped straight back again as I felt the timbers trembling under my feet. The hand-rail shook, too. I looked straight ahead. Twenty, thirty yards to the far end. Eyes fixed on where the shingle road began again, I moved forward, one pace at a time. Three . . . four . . . five. I sensed Whina standing behind me.

Nine . . . ten . . . eleven. The distant yelling grew louder. I saw black smoke pouring upwards from further down the valley. A fire. Someone's coal-range, I guessed, split open by the earthquake.

Fourteen . . . fifteen. I was almost halfway. I turned, clinging to the hand-rail. Whina stood motionless where I'd left her. She raised a hand. I faced the far end again; took another step. Seventeen . . . eighteen.

In the riverbed below, the pukeko stormed upwards once more. At the same moment, I felt it coming: a quivering through the bridge, a groaning as cables began to strain. The timber bucked. Just a dozen yards ahead, I saw the road and paddock surge as if a wave had run through them.

I clutched the hand-rail with all my strength. The whole deck lifted, hung in mid-air for half a second, then slammed down. My forehead thumped into the rail's rough wood. I screamed. Three steps in front, a section of deck graunched, splintered, and toppled towards the river.

My body hunched in terror. Sweat slid down my face. I couldn't move.

The far bank was scarred with slips where shrubs and trees had torn away. As I stared at it, I remembered my father fighting his way up there with his maimed leg, swinging the axe to help him. *He'd* kept going.

Away to one side, the silvery mist still hung over the swamp, and the hawk hovered. I took one hand off the rail, and reached forward again. One step. Two. The broken stretch of deck was right in front of me. It was forty feet straight down to the riverbed boulders. The Waimoana churned on; a big willow branch swung by on its surface, shredded where it had been torn from the bank.

I squeezed my feet into the gaps between the side supports and pulled myself along, yawning space below me. Grip. Step. Grip. Step. A voice grunted 'Come on! Come on!' Grip. Step.

My feet touched something different, and I gasped. I looked down, and I was standing on the deck. The broken section lay behind me.

I tried to sprint for the far end. My legs wouldn't work properly, and I staggered instead, reeling forward over the creaking timbers. I glimpsed pines and willows swinging; realised it wasn't just me.

I reached the road. My body sagged; I hunched, hands on knees. I couldn't believe what I'd done. Sweat was sliding down one cheek; I swiped a hand over it, stared at the blotches of red on my palm, and remembered my forehead thumping into the rail.

The black smoke kept rising in the distance. Another voice had started shouting, from behind me. Whina was laughing and cheering. She thrust a finger towards my house; then she was off, running in the direction of the pa.

★

I was off, too, tearing along the shingle road, over the stile, through the paddock where two of our cows, Raspberry and Blackberry, stood together, snorting and shivering. A raw split showed on one of the macrocarpa trunks. I flung open the back gate and stopped. Two walls of our outside lavatory had collapsed, its wooden seat perched crookedly over the hole it had taken Dad nearly a day to dig. Squares of newspaper hung neatly from the wire hook nearby. Could have been embarrassing for somebody, my stupid mind sniggered.

I hurried around the corner of the hedge. This time, my breathing stopped as well.

Mum and Dad and Nana Aggie were crouched on the lawn, Little Angus between them. Mum's eyes were shut, and my young brother shook with sobs. My father stared at where our house had split apart. A whole side wall had disappeared, and I could see right inside.

The wooden butter-boxes where I kept my clothes lay toppled and scattered across the floor. In the next room, a roof beam had snapped in half and landed across my parents' bed. The doors of their wardrobe hung wide open; the clothes inside hung in a neat row. Somehow that looked strangest of all.

I stepped forward, and Dad saw me. 'Florence! You're all right! Look, Lily. She's here. She's safe!'

He stared harder, began to say something else. My mother, who'd started struggling to her feet, clapped a hand over her mouth and gasped. I remembered my forehead. 'It's all right,' I managed to say. 'Banged my head on the side of—' But I didn't finish the sentence, because both of them flung their arms around me, holding me so hard that my breath went *Ooofff!* Nana Aggie felt her way across the lawn towards our voices, touching my sore forehead gently.

'You came back across the bridge?' Dad asked. I nodded. 'Oh, Florence,' Mum murmured. She licked her handkerchief; dabbed at the dried blood on my face. Nana Aggie smiled. 'Well done, my dear.'

Suddenly I felt so full of love for them all that I thought I might burst out crying. But I didn't, because Little Angus had just started bawling *his* head off.

For an hour, we sat on the lawn, close together, while the ground twitched and muttered. Angus had stopped crying, but he wouldn't let go of Mum's apron. I stared at the house. The kitchen was wrecked. The front porch and nearly every window had gone. But we're all right, I kept telling myself. We're all right.

'Whina?' Mum asked after a while.

'She's OK. She was heading home. We lost a sugar-bag, though. It fell in the river. Sorry. The rest are still in the orchard.'

My mother smiled. 'I think we can manage without the sugar-bag.'

'Huh!' grunted Angus. 'I was looking forward to some plums. Girls are useless!' He gave me a wobbly grin.

The shakes were further apart now, and less powerful. The trees and hedge had stopped swaying. Blackberry or Raspberry gave an 'I'm all right; how about milking me?' moo from the paddock.

Dad stood. 'I'd better check the fences. Let's have a look inside the house first.'

We can *already* look inside a lot of it, I thought. The rest of us followed my father as he limped towards the back door. He turned the handle, pushed, and the door fell flat onto the kitchen floor. Total silence for a second, then we were all gasping and laughing.

Every shelf in the kitchen had collapsed. Broken jars of fruit and jam lay everywhere. 'Oh well, the stove still looks all right,' sighed my mother. I remembered that column of black smoke rising down the valley. Whose place was it?

Dad put an arm around Mum; nodded at the splintered walls. 'We've certainly got plenty of firewood for it.' The ground shook again; Angus gripped my hand.

More time passed. I helped Mum make a pot of tea. 'I hope the chooks aren't too scared to lay eggs,' she muttered. Nana Aggie's groping hands found a loaf of bread. 'I baked that just yesterday,' she announced, blowing dust from it.

Dad stood in my parents' half-wrecked bedroom, chopping at the beam that lay across their bed. He lifted the axe, wiped its gleaming blade with his palm. 'Knew I was right to hang onto this. I'll have to tell Hahona.'

He and Angus and I lifted the bed out onto the lawn. Mum came through the gate from the paddock, holding half-a-dozen speckled eggs in her apron. 'The hayshed's all right. Just one bale fallen down, and Blackberry's already eaten half of it, the greedy thing.'

Nana Aggie was peeling potatoes at one end of the kitchen table, where it stood with the summer sun glowing down on it. 'We can sleep in the barn, then. That's what John and I did, the first few years we were married.'

Horses' hooves scrunched on the road. A voice called. Whina.

She came hurrying through our front gate. Wrong:

she came hurrying through the gap where our front gate used to be. It lay flat on the ground, just like our kitchen door. The fence on either side was a buckled line of leaning white pickets. Her mother Ahorangi followed close behind.

My friend hugged me. 'Told you we'd find you.'

Ahorangi meanwhile was embracing my mother and Nana Aggie. The little green pekapeka bat around her neck glowed in the sunlight. I looked, and yes, Mum was wearing her bracelet.

'We rode across the river just up from the pa,' Whina told me. 'There's a whole lot of willows fallen and blocked the old bed. But we managed.'

My mother held Ahorangi's hand. 'You're women! Women can manage anything, remember?'

'They can't manage to bring the plums home,' Angus piped up.

My father shook Ahorangi's other hand. Then he shook Whina's. I'd never seen him treat her so like an adult before. I guess she and I had both grown up a fair bit in the past couple of hours.

'Rawiri?' Dad asked. 'Hahona? And the pa?'

'They are safe,' Ahorangi told him. 'So are most of our whares.' She nodded towards our wrecked home. 'They are not as heavy as your pakeha houses. They do not break things if they fall.' She placed a hand on my sore forehead. 'Whina has said how you crossed the bridge. Brave girl.'

'*Two* brave girls.' Nana Aggie's unseeing eyes smiled at me.

'We came to see if you need anything,' went Ahorangi. 'Is there—'

My father was laughing. He shook his head as we stared at him. 'My grandfather — Big Angus — used to tell us stories about how they would all have starved when they first landed in New Zealand, if it weren't for the Maori people helping them. Half a century on, and it's still the same. What would we do without you?'

Whina and I wandered across the lawn, and stood staring into my ruined bedroom. 'It looks like a bomb went off.'

The ground shuddered once more. Our house's (our half-house's) side wall sagged further towards us, and we both jumped back. From the paddock, Blackberry or Raspberry gave another 'Mooo!'

Mum made more tea, pushing broken bits of house into the stove. She and Ahorangi and Nana Aggie began sorting through the mess of spilt things on the kitchen floor, Nana's hands searching expertly through the rubble.

The rest of us carried clothes and blankets to the hayshed. 'It's going to be like a picnic!' Little Angus exclaimed as he staggered along with a tin basin of soap and toothbrushes. 'Bags I sleep on the bales up under the rafters!' Whina and I rolled our eyes at each other.

We'd drunk our tea, some potatoes were boiling on the stove, and a few mutton chops that Mum had saved from the smashed meat safe were cooking in a pan. She and Dad were planning to take Nana Aggie up to the cemetery, to see if our great-grandparents' graves were all right. 'And to show them *we're* all right,' said Nana.

'Will you stay for dinner?' Mum asked Whina and Ahorangi, just like any polite posh lady. 'I'm sorry I can't spread the best table-cloth.' Everyone laughed. It had been a day of jokes as well as terror.

Ahorangi took my mother's hand again. 'No, thank you. Rawiri and his mother will start worrying about us.' She turned to Dad. 'Rawiri rides to town tomorrow, if he can. He will send telegrams to tell people we are safe. Do you—'

My father nodded. 'Yes, please. Could he send one to Jess up in Auckland? Tell her we're safe, too.'

Nana Aggie chuckled. 'Perhaps the earthquake was Jess getting angry with some politicians? That daughter of mine can usually make the ground shake.'

Another voice called from the front gate — the front gap. 'Hello? Anybody home?' Whina and I glanced at each other. She started brushing the dust from her dress, and I started trying to tidy my hair. I saw Mum and Ahorangi smiling at us.

Robert McDougall came around the wrecked side of the house. He stared at it, then at us. He held a big brown paper bag. 'Dad said to come and see if you're all right. We're fine — except he stabbed his finger with the nib of his pen when the quake came.' Robert gave a shaky laugh. 'And our kitchen caught fire, but we put it out.' I remembered that black smoke as I stumbled across the bridge.

He looked taller. It sounds silly, because I saw him just about every day at school. But he looked more . . . more like a man, somehow.

Dad was shaking his hand, just like he'd shaken Whina's. 'Glad you're safe. Tell your mother and father I'll come to see them tomorrow. We all need to stick together just now.'

Robert held out the paper bag. 'Mum said to bring these. They all fell off in the quake.' He saw our puzzled faces, and explained. 'Plums.'

Plums. I thought of the orchard, the vanished sugar-bag. I began to laugh, and knew I was nearly crying. Mum put her arms around me. Robert stared.

'See?' Little Angus was exclaiming meanwhile. 'Told you it takes a boy to manage some things!' Robert stared at him, too. He must be thinking the quake had driven us all nuts.

The ground was still. The sun had slid lower. The afternoon was warm and quiet. I could hear magpies warbling somewhere. Probably telling their cousins how they'd started the earthquake to scare us humans away.

Happiness brimmed up in me. Yes, happiness. The house didn't matter; we'd fix it or build another. I'd lived through the scariest thing I could imagine, and I was fine. So were the people I loved, and that was such a . . . a treasure.

Robert McDougall gave me a smile, then glanced away. Gosh, I hope — I hope it's not my best friend that he likes!

ALAN
1957

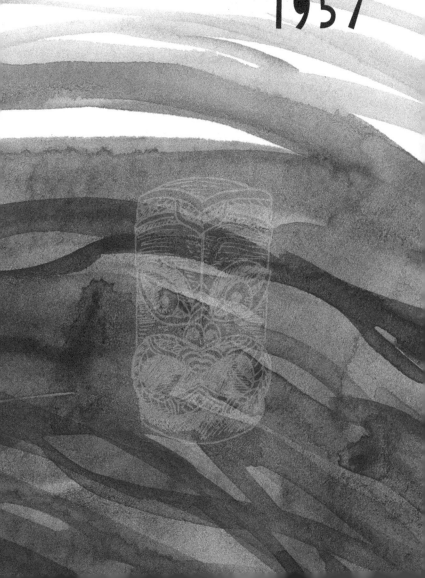

It had been raining for a week. Sheets and curtains of rain pouring down on our valley. Ridges had slipped onto side roads, and farms up in the hills were cut off. Creeks flowing into the Waimoana had burst their banks, or were dammed up by slips. In some places, only trucks and tractors could get through.

That wasn't a problem for Mum, since she can drive a truck *or* a tractor. 'I'm a woman, remember, Matiu?' I heard her saying to my dad this morning. 'We can do anything.'

I knew Dad was grinning as he replied. 'Florence, I'll never forget you're a woman. You go out there and show this weather who's boss.' So she's heading off today sometime to check on old Mrs Ross up the valley.

The rain was incredible. Mum booted my cousin Tipene and me out of the house for an hour on Monday afternoon, when it was just streaming down and not crashing down. The Waimoana charged along, all brown and powerful. Branches whirled on its surface, crashing into the rocks just upstream from the swing-bridge, then hurtling on again. We could hear the booming water from fifty yards away. As we stepped onto the deck and peered over the side, there were other noises, too: a grinding and rumbling, deep down in the river.

'Boulders,' Tipene went. 'The river's shoving them along.'

I nodded. 'Imagine Grandad Duncan trying to get across there today.'

My grandfather almost cut his leg off about 40 years ago, when he was chopping down bush to start our orchard. He says Grandma Lily and Great-aunt Jess saved his life. He's still got the axe, by the way. Well, sort of. I'll tell you more about it later.

Mum told Tipene and me the story a couple of days ago, as the rain thrashed down. I'd heard it before, but I was so bored after being stuck inside (during the holidays, too!) that I'd listen to anything. And she's a good story-teller.

Tipene and I are second cousins, six times removed, says Mum. We're related way back. We're best mates, too, just like our mothers. Our birthdays are in the same month; we both turn thirteen at the end of this year. My mum and Auntie Whina have known each other since they started school. For a while, they even liked the same boy — our teacher, Mr McDougall Junior. Hard to imagine a teacher being a boy. Even harder to imagine girls liking him. But Mum says he was really good-looking and thoughtful, and she started thinking Whina and she might end up fighting to see who got him. I'd like to have seen that!

Then my father, Matiu, arrived. Mum took one look at him, and that was it. 'Well, I was so handsome,' Dad grinned. 'And charming. And clever. And—' Mum punched him in the ribs. '—and lucky, dear,' he went. So Auntie Whina married Mr McDougall Junior — Uncle Robert — and Mum married . . . Dad.

My father used to live where a lot of people in our pa came from, ages ago. He's called Matiu Fergus Hohepa, because his own father was Maori and his mother was Scottish, from the families that came out here, ages ago, too. My mum says that when they were married, in St Peter's Church not far from the pa, one of Mum's uncles got ready to play his bagpipes as she and Dad came out. As soon as they saw the pipes, Nana Ahorangi and other old people stuck their hands over their ears and started laughing. There's a story how when people here heard bagpipes the first time, they thought it was a taniwha — a monster.

'Fair enough,' Dad said. 'Your mother reckons *I'm* a monster.'

My father came to our valley because he'd been at university, studying archaeology: ancient history and old ruins and stuff. He started hearing the legends about treasure maybe hidden in the swamp beside the Waimoana, so he wanted to talk to the old folk at the pa, and maybe do some exploring.

Then he met Mum, who was visiting Whina. 'And that was the end of my archaeology, Alan. You make sure you study something where you don't meet any gorgeous young women.'

I haven't a clue what I'll study. I like farming. I like reading. I don't like girls much; they're a pain. I'm glad I don't have to put up with a sister like Tipene does, though I suppose Finola's not too bad. But I wouldn't have minded a brother. Anyway, I won't worry about what to study until I start high school next term. Tipene wants us to take the same subjects. 'We mongrel guys gotta stick together!'

Mongrel? Dad's half-caste: part-Maori, part-Pakeha. Mum's all Pakeha, so that makes me quarter-caste. Auntie Whina is Maori, and Uncle Robert McDougall is Pakeha, so that makes Tipene half-caste. 'We sound like fruit salads!' Finola said when we were talking about it one time.

Their parents got married before mine did. The bagpipes played again, and no taniwha rang up to complain. But soon after, Uncle Robert got called up to fight in World War Two. He was an artilleryman in the North African desert and in Italy. Auntie Whina told Mum she felt terrified every time someone knocked on the door, in case it was a message from the Army to say he was wounded or dead. Nana Ahorangi gave her the greenstone bat then, to protect them both.

But Uncle Robert (I try not to call him that at school) did come home safely. Phew!

The rain was falling even harder. At our place, Tipene and I had played all the card games we knew: Snap, and Sevens, and Five Hundred. At his place, we'd read books and listened to wireless serials: *Dad and Dave,* about life on an Australian outback farm; *Dossier on Dumetrius,* a spy story. Tipene taught me some more Maori words. He and Finola have learned lots from Auntie Whina. She taught our class some.

There's no Maori language taught at high school, which I reckon is pathetic. There was an argument in the paper about it. One woman wrote that Maori was a dying language and not spoken anywhere else in the world, so kids should be taught Latin instead. My parents and Tipene's wrote a letter saying Latin wasn't a dying language; it was a *dead* language, and if New

Zealand schools taught Maori, it would help make that language healthy again. The letter had all their names on, and it looked really good.

★

Since I'm quarter-caste and Tipene's half-caste, there are some things we can't do. If he ever becomes an All Black (and he's really good at sport), he won't be able to go to South Africa, because black people and white people can't play sport against one another there. They're kept apart other ways, too. Well, even in New Zealand, there are places that don't like having Maori or part-Maori people. We had trouble one time in town just a few months back.

'You feel more like a Maori or a Pakeha?' Tipene asked yesterday — Tuesday, when we wandered down to the river again. The rain had lifted a bit, and Auntie Whina had chucked us out, just like Mum did on Monday.

I stared. 'Dunno. Neither, really.' Most of the time I just feel like . . . like Alan Hohepa. I'm Pakeha, and I'm Maori, and I'm OK being both.

Tipene's darker than me, but we're the same height, and people seem to guess we're related. 'How about you?' I asked. 'What do you feel like most?'

He shrugged. 'Depends.' We stood at the start of the

ridge, watching the river storming past below. A chunk of bank had been ripped away; a raw gouge of clay the size of a house glistened.

Tipene gazed upstream towards the swamp, where floodwaters gleamed among the flax and reeds. 'Sometimes I feel mostly Maori, like when Nana Ahorangi and Grandad Rawiri are telling me about special places like that.' He jerked his head at the swamp. 'Or in bad ways, like that milk bar. And sometimes I feel more Pakeha, like when we're doing Maths and stuff at school. Or when I'm with some useless sort-of-white guy called Alan.'

So I punched him on the shoulder, and he punched me on the arm, and we both laughed. We gazed down at the roaring Waimoana. 'Wonder if that was how the river at Tangiwai looked that time?' I said. 'The Whangaehu?'

Tipene nodded, and we both stood silent for a bit. A black tree-trunk showed for a second in the racing current, then vanished. No, not a tree-trunk: a dead cow. Dad had been telling Grandad Duncan on the phone this morning how the creeks and rivers were getting higher every hour. Some sheep and cattle had been swept away. I wouldn't want to be in the river today.

The rain had started again, although the sky looked a bit lighter in the west: dark grey instead of black grey. We turned to head back towards the house.

My Uncle Angus was killed four years ago. 'Little Angus' Mum called him, even though he was a tall, strong guy. 'Big Angus' was my great-great-great-grandad; he's buried up in the cemetery, with lots of my other rellies.

My uncle was on the night express train heading to Auckland, on Christmas Eve 1953. He'd met a woman in Auckland while he was studying up there (he wanted to be a soil scientist, and help farmers grow more without harming the land), and they were planning to get married. He'd been down to visit my parents and grandparents, show them her photo, tell them all about her.

It was late at night, and his train was passing near Mount Ruapehu. What nobody knew was that the crater lake on the mountain had filled with so much water that the crater walls couldn't hold it back any longer.

About an hour before the express train was due to pass, the crater collapsed, and a huge torrent of water, ice and boulders went hurtling down the side of Ruapehu and into the Whangaehu River. It tore downstream 'like a battering ram', the papers said, and smashed into the bridge where road and railway crossed. The bridge broke apart and was swept away.

A man driving north reached the bridge, saw the thundering river, and realised what had happened. At the same moment, he glimpsed the train's headlight as it sped towards the bridge. He sprinted for the railway line, waving his torch. The driver must have seen something, because he slammed on his brakes. But the express couldn't stop in time, and the engine, plus half a dozen carriages crashed down into the water.

Over 150 people died, and my uncle was one of them. Some survivors saw him dragging people through the carriages' broken windows, pushing them towards the bank. Then one carriage flipped over, and a wall of water swept him away. They found his body the next day, half a mile downstream. He's buried in our cemetery, too.

I was only nine, but I remember my mother and Nana Lily crying and crying. Grandad Duncan went out, carrying the axe that he'd hurt himself with that time, and began chopping at an old macrocarpa tree that he'd been trimming for firewood. He chopped so hard that the axe broke. He came back to the farmhouse holding the handle.

Uncle Angus was buried a week later. Auntie Whina laid her greenstone bat on the grave, and left it there for a week. Nana Lily did the same with her silver bracelet; then afterwards she gave it to Mum. Some people were afraid that the magpies would steal them, but they lay there untouched.

★

Tipene and I sloshed along the shingle road towards the stile leading into our home paddock. I was thinking about the milk bar he'd mentioned: I'll never forget that.

We were in town one day last year. Auntie Whina and Mum wanted new shoes, even though Uncle Robert and Dad said there were plenty of decent gumboots around. They gave me and Tipene and Finola money to buy a milkshake each while they were in the shop — 'and to stop you boys being silly while we choose'.

The guy serving in the milk bar watched us come in. Finola asked, 'Could I have a vanilla milkshake, please?' Tipene went 'I'll have a chocolate one, thanks', and I said 'Me, too.'

The guy behind the counter didn't answer for a couple of seconds, then he muttered 'Not serving just now'.

We boys stared at him. When Finola spoke again, her voice sounded tight. 'We'd like to buy our milkshakes, please.'

The man shook his head, went 'Not serving' again. 'Try Wilson's.'

Wilson's Milk Bar is right down the far end of town. I couldn't work out what he was on about. But Finola and Tipene had realised something. My friend's hands were clenched into fists. Finola's face had gone hot and angry. She's three years older than him, almost sixteen then, and she stood there like a grown-up. Her eyes stayed on the guy serving — *not* serving. He wouldn't look at her; started wiping the counter.

After another few seconds, Finola went 'You're pathetic. You know that?' She turned and strode out. Tipene glared at the guy, then followed. I went after them, trying to understand what was going on.

'What—' I began when we were out on the footpath. But right then, Finola put her hands to her face and burst into tears. Tipene looked wilder than I'd ever seen him.

'What—' I began again, like a cuckoo clock or something.

My friend glared at me. 'He wouldn't serve any of us because we're Maori. Couldn't you tell? The bloody pig!'

My mouth dropped open. I felt my own face start to heat up.

Finola pulled out her handkerchief (how come girls always have a clean handkerchief?), and swiped it across her eyes. 'He— He—'

Right then, Mum and Auntie Whina came out of the shoe shop across the road. They weren't carrying any shopping bags, so maybe they'd decided on the gumboots after all. Auntie Whina saw her daughter crying on the opposite footpath and charged over to her, while cars slammed their brakes on.

Finola dragged in deep breaths and told her mother what had happened. 'He told us to go to Wilson's instead,' Tipene said. My friend's fists were still clenched. I heard Mum make a hissing sound through her teeth.

Auntie Whina held Finola's hand. She's shorter than Mum, but she seemed to have grown six inches taller. 'We're going to be very polite, darling.' Then mother and daughter stalked into the milk bar, with the rest of us trailing behind.

The guy behind the counter glanced up, and his mouth opened. Auntie Whina strode to the counter and gazed at him for a second. She spoke in a voice so sweet, I hardly recognised it.

'Good morning. I believe my daughter and son and their friend wanted a milkshake a few minutes ago, and you wouldn't serve them. Is that right?'

The man's head was down. He kept wiping the counter, which didn't need wiping.

Auntie Whina waited a moment, then: 'I think you owe them an apology. I'd like to hear it — now.'

The guy's face twisted. He opened his mouth. Right then, my mother stepped forward so she stood beside Auntie Whina. 'If you don't apologise, I'll write to the paper and ring the radio station. I'm sure they'll be interested to hear what you did.'

The man's cheeks were blotched with red. He muttered something. I think I heard the word 'sorry'.

Auntie Whina's eyes stayed fixed on him. 'I suppose that feeble effort is all we'll get from someone like you. Well, you'll be sorrier still. None of my friends or my whanau — you're probably too ignorant to know that word — will ever buy anything from here again.'

'That goes for my friends and family, too,' went Mum. The two women stood side by side; the guy scowled at the floor. 'You're going to lose dozens of customers,' my mother went on. 'You deserve it for being such a bigot. Wilson's will make a fortune.'

She put an arm around Auntie Whina, who was still holding Finola's hand. The three of them turned and strode from the milk bar. Tipene and I straggled after them. 'Wow!' my friend breathed to me. His eyes gleamed.

Yeah, I thought, really intelligently. Wow!

That slightly lighter stretch of grey cloud to one side had grown a bit by the time Tipene and I reached our farmhouse and started taking off our oilskins on the back porch. But the rain still fell. Our cows stood in the shelter of the remaining macrocarpas, slowly chewing their cud and looking thoughtful, like cows do.

We went down the hall to my room, past the photo of Great-aunt Jess wearing her MBE. It stands for

Member of the British Empire, and it's a flash medal on a flash ribbon that she got for helping poor people, ages and ages ago. She'd have been proud of what Mum and Auntie Whina did in the milk bar.

'That you, boys?' Mum called from the kitchen. 'Come say hello to Nana and Grandad.'

She and my grandparents sat around the big table. Grandad Duncan's axe handle leaned against his chair. He uses it as a walking stick when his leg hurts him. He reckons he's got plans for the handle, whatever that means.

We talked while Tipene and I scoffed scones. 'How's the orchard looking?' Grandad wanted to know. 'Flood isn't up that far, is it?'

We told him it wasn't. Our family still picks fruit from his orchard, even though it's easy to drive into town and get things now — especially since we've got one of those flash new grocery shops where you serve yourself. 'I'm not leaving it all to those cheeky magpies,' Grandad says.

Just to show it wasn't finished, the rain crashed down again as we ate the last scones and headed to my room. We gave Great-aunt Jess (MBE)'s photo a pretend salute as we went past. When she visited us about four years ago, she and Nana Ahorangi went shopping in town for a posh dress. The shop had a snooty saleswoman who looked Tipene's nana up and down, and asked 'Is it for anything special?'

'Yes,' went Great-aunt Jess with a sweet smile. 'My friend and I are meeting the Governor-General.' The saleswoman's mouth dropped open like a fish.

It was true. After World War Two, people in our valley got together and raised money to build a Memorial Hall to the men and women from around here who fought in the two world wars. Great-aunt Jess wrote to Government House in Wellington, saying it would be good if the Governor-General could come and open it. He did!

He was a tall bloke with a Pommy accent and a suit. Tipene and I felt a bit disappointed. We thought he might wear a robe and carry a sword or something. Our school did a special welcome and haka that Auntie Whina and Uncle Robert (should I call him that?) had taught us. And Nana Ahorangi wore her posh dress.

In my room, Tipene and I played Snap a few more times. The sky outside was getting lighter; there'd only been a couple of showers after that last heavy fall. Maybe we could go and have a really good look at the river.

Nearly a week stuck inside, and, like I said, it was the holidays.

Just after lunch, Mum called out: 'I'm off to see old Mrs Ross. You boys OK?'

It was Tipene who replied. 'I'd better be getting home, Auntie Florence. Thanks for letting me stay.' Straightaway I went: 'Can I go with Tipene?'

'All right,' Mum replied. 'But stay away from the river. It'll be really dangerous for a few days.' When we said nothing, she called 'You hear me?'

'Uh-huh,' we both went. We didn't look at each other.

Mum left a few minutes later. Our truck bounced off down the drive, a couple of haybales still in its tray. Tipene and I put on our gumboots and oilskins once more, and headed off towards the bridge. We didn't lock the door; nobody in our valley worries about stuff like that.

Drizzle still drifted down, but a lot of the sky was just light grey now. We reached the bridge, and stood looking at the Waimoana bulldozing along, filling its whole bed, more branches spinning in the water as it tore by. A thin sunlight touched the swamp upstream. Reeds, flax, the water among them gleamed silver. A hawk hung above, the way it always does, like a sentry guarding something.

'Great, eh?' Tipene murmured.

It was. The swamp always looks magic. Dad reckons the hair on his neck stood on end the first time he went there, and he soon gave up any idea of digging for anything. It just didn't feel right, he said.

We gazed up and down the valley. The orchard trees glittered with raindrops. The paddocks lay silent, pools of water dotted across them. The hawk wheeled. I'm going to stay here forever, I decided. I'm going to be a farmer and live here, and keep all my Pakeha and Maori friends, and it'll be absolutely amazing. I blinked. Where did all that come from so suddenly?

Like I said before, I hadn't really thought about what I was going to be. I knew we'd learn about jobs when we started high school — just a few weeks away! But the main thing Tipene and I were interested in was the high-school army cadets. You get a proper army uniform, and do marching and training for a week. You even get to shoot (only at targets) with proper .303 rifles.

But now this thought had hit me. I blinked again, then followed Tipene along the wooden deck. The river boomed past, forty feet below; the bridge trembled. I thought of that dead cow; anything falling in there wouldn't have a hope. I wondered if there'd been any more slips on the streams further up the valley.

Finola already knows what she's going to do when she leaves high school. She sat her School Certificate exams at the end of last year. You have to get 200 marks before they'll let you into the Sixth Form, and she swotted really hard. Typical girl. She's got a holiday job three days a week at the district council office in town, and she wants to be a teacher. Fancy wanting that!

She said she felt nervous before her job interview. Ever since that milk-bar business, she's ready for people to snub her because she's part-Maori. But the council offered her the holiday job straightaway.

Nobody's ever picked on me for my race, except for a couple of guys at school after Tipene and I told them to stop taking the cricket gear that Standard Three and Four used at lunchtime. One of them went 'Aw yeah, you Horis always stick together, eh?' I didn't take much notice, but Tipene was pretty wild.

Beneath the deck, the Waimoana roared past so loudly we had to raise our voices to hear each other. Just upstream, the big shelves of rock where we like to swim were half underwater. You could see water foaming beneath the ledge that was our secret hiding place when we were little.

'Let's have a look, eh?' Tipene pointed at the rocks.

'Yeah, good idea.' I remembered Mum telling us to stay away from the river. But, well, we wouldn't be in the river — we'd be on the bank above it. So we climbed over the fence, and headed towards the rocks. A gigantic willow branch came hurtling down on the frothing water. It rammed into the bank, and lifted straight up in the air. Then it thwacked back down into the current, and went spinning on.

'Hey!' Tipene yelled.

'Hey!' I yelled, too; original as always.

We grinned at each other. It's hard to believe anyone could look down on Tipene and Finola and their family, or any of us, for being Maori. But I'd woken up a bit to some things, especially when we talked at school about the rugby tour.

Last year — 1956 — the Springboks toured New Zealand, and the All Blacks beat them, three test matches to one! It was the first time we'd ever won a series against South Africa. We all listened to the games on the wireless, and when New Zealand won the final test, Mum and Dad and I cheered and yelled.

Since South Africa keeps its black and white people apart, there were no black players in the Springbok team. And if the All Blacks tour there, they can't take any Maori players.

We couldn't believe it when Mr McDougall told us.

Kids started going 'That's rotten!' 'I hate that.' 'We should take our Maori blokes anyway!' 'Yeah, we play better than you Pakeha jokers, too!' (That last one was Tipene, of course.) The class got quite noisy, until Mr McDougall held up a hand, and we all went quiet again.

'It's something you might like to talk about with your parents,' our teacher said. 'How do they feel about it?' Actually, some people in the valley reckon we shouldn't let political things interfere with rugby, and the All Blacks should go without Maori players. My dad — my Maori dad! — says if we tour there, then South African teams will keep touring here, and they can learn how different races get along. I don't agree . . . I think.

We squelched along the path towards the rocks, past where a road-mender used to live years ago. His hut fell down in the big earthquake when Mum was just a few years older than I am now. She must have been pretty brave, getting across the bridge to reach home. They had to build a whole new deck later.

Funny thing is, the earthquake made some good things happen. Before then, my Great-great-aunt Janet had sort of cut herself off from the family. There'd been an argument, and she moved away. But after the quake, she got back in touch to see if everyone was all right, even came to visit. Strange how things change, eh? See, I'm a poet as well as an original thinker.

We can see our farmhouse from the rocks. When we're swimming there, we sometimes wave and call out to Dad or Grandad Duncan if they're in the paddocks.

We reached the edge of the bank and stopped. The water stampeded past, ten feet below. It crashed against the bank, sprayed up onto the ledge, and swept across the rocks. A square piece of wood lay there, where the flood must have landed it. Another branch, a small one, flashed past on a whirling eddy. It sped on downstream, faster than a person could run.

'Look at that!' Tipene said — shouted, actually. I *was* looking. This was amazing. I'd never known water could have so much power in it.

Above us, a couple of patches of blue gleamed for a second, then disappeared. The rain had almost stopped. Maybe the farms upriver wouldn't have suffered too badly after all. I wondered how many streams had been blocked by slips.

Tipene was saying something, but I couldn't hear him over the roar of the river. A grinding sound swelled, then faded. More boulders being dragged along in the current. 'What?' I asked.

'Let's go down. Be great to see it up close.'

I stared around. The sky was clearing over the swamp. The Waimoana seemed to have reached right into the flax and reeds. The door of our hayshed stood open, but nobody was in sight.

Yeah, we could climb down and stand on the rocks that the water was sweeping across. It was fast, but only ankle-deep. If we held onto the sides of the bank, we'd be fine. OK, Mum had told us not to, but we wouldn't be in the dangerous part.

My friend was already out of his oilskin and kicking off his gumboots. I took another look around, then started taking off my boots and coat as well. We piled them on top of the bank.

Tipene began clambering down. There were handholds — a stone, a hollow in the bank, a tree root — that we used when we went there to swim. I followed. The clay was muddy; I'd have to be careful not to get too much on my clothes, or Mum would want to know where we'd been.

My feet touched something. 'Don't tread on my head!' Tipene yelled. He was a poet, too? He stared at the water sweeping across the stony surface below him, looking for a place to put his own feet.

'Why not?' I called back. 'Your head's harder than a rock!' We both started sniggering.

Tipene reached a leg down. Then he was standing, the muddy water sluicing around his shins. He staggered for a moment, grabbed at the bank, and said, 'It's OK. Come down.'

I let go of the root I was holding, reached down for a hollow in the bank, and followed. The clay was so sodden, it came away in my hand. I half-lurched, half-dropped onto the rock beside my friend, clutching at him as I did so. We both reeled sideways, then stood with the water skimming past.

'You've ruined that handhold.' Tipene stared at the gouge in the bank where clay had slumped away. 'We'll have to get back up a different way.'

I took no notice. I pointed at the small ledge, our hiding place. 'What's that?'

Tipene turned to look. I heard his breath stop.

The square piece of wood was just a few feet away. We were close enough to see the shapes on its side. Whorls, curves, a face with a tongue pushed out. Silver and blue glowed. A pair of paua-shell eyes, set into the wood.

Tipene's voice was hushed, but I could hear him above the rush of water. 'The river left it there. It's — it must have come from the swamp.'

'Let's see.' I began edging towards it, bracing myself against the bank with both hands. The water only reached up to my ankles here, but it was so fast, so full of power, that it tugged me sideways. We stared at the dark wooden shape wedged on the ledge just ahead. I could see more details now: raised hands, legs astride, patterns like tree-trunks at the sides.

I sloshed forward another step. 'Be careful,' Tipene muttered.

'It's OK. The water's shallow.'

My friend shook his head. 'I don't mean that.' His eyes were fixed on the carving just three steps away; his lips were parted.

I gazed at the carving again, and a shiver ran through my body. The paua eyes seemed to glitter straight at me.

The river surged, and washed around my shins. I gripped the bank harder. Another step. I started to crouch, still bracing myself with one hand, reaching for the carving.

Then I paused. I straightened up and moved aside. I heard myself speaking to Tipene. 'You — you take it.'

It must have sounded stupid, like I was scared or something. But my friend just nodded once. His eyes stayed on the carving. I thought I heard him murmur something in Maori, and words he'd taught me were in my head, too. He stooped and reached both hands forward, took hold of the little panel gently, easing it out of the crack just above the ledge, where the Waimoana had swept it. He stayed crouched for a few seconds, holding it. Then, very slowly, he rose to his feet.

The water frothed over our ankles. Just a couple of

yards away, the river crashed past, gouging at the bank. But around us, everything seemed to have gone silent.

The carving . . . Whorls and diamond patterns. Rows of tiny teeth shapes, each one exactly the same size. One of the hands held a club, just like a picture Mr McDougall had shown us at school once. Even that was covered with tiny scrolls and circles. The other hand rested across the figure's stomach. The wood was dark with water, but it seemed to glow golden under the grey sky. The silver-blue eyes glittered, and I realised Tipene's hand was trembling.

He turned to gaze at me. Neither of us spoke, but I knew that even if I lived to be 200 (OK, not likely), I'd never forget this moment. And I felt so pleased we'd found it together.

My friend began to speak, swallowed, tried again. His fingers moved across the wood, following the winding patterns. It's like the river, I realised: the shape of the river.

'I — we'll take it to Mum. To Nana Ahorangi. They'll know what to do.'

I stared at him. Do what? Yet I already half-knew what he meant. This was so special. Special people had to decide about it.

My own hand was tracing the whorls and little diamond patterns. The current tugged harder at our feet, and I lurched slightly. Upstream, the Waimoana rumbled louder. Time we got out of here, before someone saw us and we got in deep trouble. Hell, we were going to get in trouble anyway; we'd have to explain how we got hold of this. Yet trouble didn't seem to matter just now.

Tipene drew in a deep breath, grinned at me. 'Incredible, eh? It's just—'

Paaarrp! Paaarrp! From across the other side of the valley, a horn blared twice, loud and harsh. The two of us burst out laughing.

'Yeah,' Tipene agreed. 'It's just *paarrp*.' As he spoke, the horn blew again, longer. Then once more. A traffic jam? Not in our valley: two trucks and a tractor going past is our idea of heavy traffic.

Tipene sighed. 'We better get going.' He turned to the bank we'd climbed down; nodded at a crack beside where the clay had come away in my grasp. 'We can get up there, if you don't wreck that handhold, too.'

'Me?' I pretended to be annoyed. 'It was you swinging down like a mad gorilla that made it come loose.'

My friend grinned. He began to tuck the carving inside his shirt. 'Typical Pakeha; making excuses.' Now we both grinned. Yeah, I'd never forget this.

Paaarrp! Paaarrp! The car or whatever it was sounded closer now. 'Aw, shut up!' I called. What were they making so much fuss about?

Paaaaarrrrrp! 'Stick a sock in it!' yelled Tipene. I pushed my feet through the water and reached for the bank. 'Yeah, I can fit my hand in—'

Then we went still.

My head swung to listen. A noise was growing upstream. A murmuring and sighing, like voices breathing out together. No, like an engine swelling louder. A train? Couldn't be.

Paaarrp! Paaaaarrrrrpp! The horn blasted again. It was closer still, nearly at our place. Actually, it sounded like our truck.

The noise upriver changed. It became a roaring *whoosh*, a rumbling. It rose to a booming. The bank I leaned against began to shudder. We stood, staring; Tipene had one hand inside his shirt, where he'd tucked the carving. And we saw it.

It was the whole width of the Waimoana, charging towards us faster than a person could run. A foaming crest of brown and white, six feet high, smashing forward between the banks, flinging itself upwards in spouts as it came.

Those slips upstream. The dams they'd formed across the other rivers feeding into ours. One of them had broken, its water tearing into the Waimoana, a tidal wave just a few seconds away from us.

A tree flew into the air, flung by the rampaging crest, then crashed back down and vanished. The force of it! It would snatch us away; we couldn't stand against it.

I spun around to the bank, trying to clutch at handholds, knowing I didn't have time to pull myself up. But Tipene seized my shoulder, yelled into my ear. He was trying to go first?

No. 'The ledge!' he shouted. 'Get onto the ledge!'

Next second, we were sloshing and scrambling onto the rocky lip where the carving had lain, squashing ourselves into the narrow cleft behind it. Stones scraped against my sides. I hunched my back, forcing myself further in, clutching at rocks jutting from the walls.

A monstrous booming filled the world. The light changed as a great sheet of muddy foam lifted above us. We braced our legs and hips against the sides. I screwed my eyes shut.

The wave slammed across the shelf where we'd been standing, and the solid stone trembled. Then we were underwater as it gushed into the gap where we huddled, shoving and ripping like some wild animal, ramming us against the walls. Sharp rock tore at my cheek.

Tipene lost his grip. I felt the river pluck at him; one arm slipped, and his body twisted sideways, out into the raging current. I snatched at him, so hard that my fingers sank into the flesh of his shoulder. He reeled back against the rocky wall of the crack; his head whacked into it. I held on, back jammed against the stony wall, hands locked onto my friend. We were still underwater. My lungs ached; the current yanked at me. Tipene sagged limply.

I had to breathe. I must. And right then, the water surged away as fast as it had covered us, and I crouched, dripping and gasping, half out of the gap. Tipene lolled in my grasp, slumping into the water that now churned around our knees.

I gulped, choked, managed to yell. 'Hold on!' My friend didn't move. 'Tipene!' I saw blood sheeting down his face from the matted hair, remembered that impact of his head against the stone.

My teeth ground together in a snarl. I set my legs against the wall and heaved. Tipene half-slithered, half-slumped up into the gap beside me. Something hard scraped my ribs: the carving inside his shirt.

My heart thudded; my breath rasped. 'Tipene! I bawled again. 'Help!' No movement. Blood poured down his cheek.

★

The river charged past. Just four steps away from where we hunched, it was still a thundering torrent, but around us it had dropped to shin-height once more. The wave from the burst dam or whatever it was had passed. But I couldn't get up the bank; if I let go of my friend, he'd collapse onto the ledge, be swept off it into the current. We were trapped.

I shook him. 'Tipene!' He hung in my grip, a dead weight.

A new terror made me cry out loud. I stared at him, tried to hear any sound of breathing, see if his chest was moving. I shoved my mouth against his face. 'Tipene! Wake up!'

He twitched and made a moaning sound. I sobbed with relief. But then his head flopped forward again. My arms and shoulders ached; I couldn't keep holding him much longer.

I clenched my teeth, tightened my grip on my injured friend, tried to shut out the pain in my own body. What could I do? No use shouting for help: the roaring flood would drown me out. Even if anyone came along the path above, they'd never see us unless they stopped and looked down. Anyway, there was no knowing what the dam-burst had done as it tore down the valley. Animals might have been swept away; people would have their hands full. It could be hours before anyone started wondering where we were.

Tipene moaned again. I shook him, shouted at him.

He stirred, then went limp once more. It was hopeless. My own body was shuddering with cold and strain.

Then I saw someone.

A figure stood in our paddock, near the hayshed. Grandad Duncan: I could see his walking stick. He seemed to be staring towards the rocks where Tipene and I were huddling.

'Grandad!' I yelled. He couldn't possibly hear me. He didn't move. Then someone else appeared, striding through the gate from our farmhouse. My father.

Had they seen us? They might just be watching the river; any second now, they'd turn and head off to check cows and fences in the lower paddocks. The two of them stood close together. My eyes were blurry with the strain of holding on to Tipene; I couldn't even be sure they were looking our way.

I had one chance. I hauled the deepest breath I could into my lungs. I clutched a fistful of my friend's soaked shirt, feeling the edge of the carving inside. I took one step out onto the ledge, and instantly, the water dragged and sucked at me. I braced myself as much as I could, then I lifted my right arm above my head, and waved it backwards and forwards in great sweeping arcs. Once . . . twice . . . three times. I groaned and whimpered with the effort.

The figures in the paddock moved. They seemed to jump, as if someone had yelled in their ears. My father's own arm flew up, and he stabbed it in our direction. Then he was rushing for the stile onto the road. Grandad began limping after him; then he turned, headed for the farmhouse.

How long would it take them? How long could I hold on? I started edging back into the gap above the ledge. A splintering noise, and I froze as a big willow branch swept past in the current, crashing and grinding against the rocks. A foot closer, and it would have scraped us off into the torrent.

I jammed my shoulder into the crack, and snatched at Tipene's belt. I was half-leaning, half-kneeling; it must have looked like I'd got him in some weird rugby tackle. He stirred once more, made a grunting sound.

'Hang on!' I panted. 'Someone's coming. Hang on!' He seemed to hear, half-lifted a hand to grip me, then flopped again.

Dad had disappeared. He must be on the bridge now, rushing towards us. Or had the bridge been smashed by that flood surge ripping through? No, it mustn't. It had to be there still, or else we'd — we'd die.

Movement in the paddock. Three more people hurrying through the farmhouse gate and across towards the stile. Mum and Auntie Whina. And Finola, swerving past the others. Grandad Duncan limped after them.

I shut my eyes; tried to hold Tipene even harder, began counting to myself. One . . . two. A swell of water burst onto us. Five . . . six. My arms and shoulders stabbed with agony. Ten . . . eleven. I couldn't hold on any longer.

'Alan!' My father's voice, right above me. 'Alan!' He crouched on the bank where we'd climbed down just ten minutes before, his face white and tense.

'Tipene's — hurt,' I grunted. Dad didn't move for a second, then he snatched at something beside him. Our oilskins. He began knotting the sleeve of mine onto one of Tipene's 'Hold on!' He tore off his own coat, knotted it to my friend's.

'I'll drop this down. Can you tie it into his belt?'

My jaw had begun to shudder so much, I couldn't speak. I jerked my head. The crazy oilskin rope swung down, landed across my shoulders. Tipene shifted; mumbled something.

'Dad's here.' My voice wobbled. 'We're going to pull you up.'

I seized the free end of the oilskins. Only my legs and body stopped Tipene from sliding into the water sweeping around my ankles. My numb fingers pushed at the stiff waterproof cloth, trying to stuff it under his belt. It wouldn't go. I yelled 'Come on!', shoved so hard I almost lost my balance, and it slipped through. I fumbled and yanked; tied it into a double knot. My friend was starting to slide down; his legs made scrabbling movements.

Someone else had arrived on the bank. Finola, wet hair all over her face, mouth open. Just as well it's one of her days off, eh? my mind told me, helpfully. She and Dad gripped the other end of the oilskin rope.

'Hold — him!' my father gasped, and began to heave. Tipene's body lurched off the ledge and thudded into the bank. I clutched at him, teetered towards the river. Finola screamed.

Tipene saved me. My hands were locked onto his belt, and I fell forward against him, my face jammed against the knotted oilskin. It'll break, I knew. It'll tear apart.

It didn't. I clutched at the bank, found a handhold, clung there. My friend's hands moved, holding himself away from the crack. His body jerked upwards. I glimpsed Dad's face — eyes slitted, teeth bared. Finola hauled beside him. Five seconds, and Tipene was sprawling safe on the grass, while my father tore at the knot around his waist.

I slumped against the bank, sucking in breaths. The

current surged around my ankles; my heart thumped. Dad was still tugging at the oilskins fixed to my friend's belt. 'Hang on, son! Just a couple of seconds.'

'Tipene!' a new voice called. 'Tipene!' Auntie Whina had arrived. She dropped on all fours beside where he was sprawled. The little greenstone bat swung from her neck. Mum was there, too, hands clasped to her face, staring down at me. Silver glinted at her wrist.

Dad kept wrestling at the knot. 'Alan!' My mother gasped. 'How—'

My neck hurt from gaping up at them. I tried to say something. Finola cut across us all. She'd half-risen to her feet, pointing upstream. 'Look! Hurry, Uncle Matiu!'

At the same moment, I heard it. The same murmuring and sighing, swelling to a whooshing. Somewhere up the valley, water had burst through another slip. A second wave was coming.

Dad flicked a look, panted 'God, no!' He stopped wrenching at the oilskin around Tipene's waist, begin ripping at the one further down. Another figure appeared beside him. Grandad Duncan, also panting, leaning on his axe-handle stick.

My body hunched. Could I cram myself back into the gap where my friend and I had huddled? I didn't have any strength left. The wave would tear me away. The whooshing grew louder. Faces stared down at me.

Grandad Duncan fell. He collapsed face-down on the bank's edge, arms hanging over. Mum called out; the others jerked towards him.

Then I realised. He was grasping one end of his axe handle, straining to push it towards me. It wasn't long enough; a whole foot too high for me to reach.

Dad threw himself down beside my grandfather, while Mum shouted 'Matiu!' He gripped Grandad Duncan with one hand; his other stretched forward, seized the wooden shaft. My grandfather thrust his chest and arms over the bank, shoving the handle down further. I glimpsed Finola and the others clutching at the two men's legs. A human ladder. The handle was almost within my reach.

The bank shook. Something huge rose in the river and thundered towards the rocks. My teeth clenched, my eyes bulged, and I hurled myself upwards.

At the same second, Dad and Grandad somehow made another lunge down. My hands seized the handle, and instantly they were yanking me up. My face rammed into the clay. The wave smashed across the rocks, swirled around my waist, plucking at me.

My hands began to slip from the wood. Then a hand snatched at my shirt, another grabbed my wrist, and I shot up over the edge of the bank like a hooked fish, thumping onto the wonderful, filthy grass.

★

They all had hold of me. Every one of them. My father and grandfather clutched my clothes; Mum and Auntie Whina pulled at my arms; Finola seized one hand, heaved so hard that I thought my fingers would pop out of their sockets. Even Tipene was trying to crawl towards me.

They stared at me as they knelt or sprawled on the grass. Their clothes were dirty and drenched. I stared back. Then I opened my mouth, and — and I burst into tears.

Yeah, I know. It's pathetic. Guys don't cry. But I lay there, water draining from me, body aching and shaking, face and chest coated with mud where they'd dragged me up the bank, and I blubbered like a little kid.

Mum crouched with her arms around me, murmuring 'Alan . . . darling' (that was pretty embarrassing, too) over and over. Auntie Whina held Tipene. An ugly gash ran from one eyebrow up into his hair; clotted blood covered half his face. He was watching me; struggling to speak. I managed a wobbly nod at him.

Finola sat beside her brother, crying even harder than I was. That made me feel better, for some reason. Dad and Grandad? They stood gazing down at us. Dad had one arm across my grandfather's shoulders. When he saw me looking, Grandad Duncan lifted the axe handle he was leaning on once more, and grinned. 'Told you I had plans for it.'

I turned towards Mum, gasped as every muscle in my neck and shoulders stabbed. 'That horn. Did—'

She laid her hand against my cheek. 'I was driving back from old Mrs Ross, and saw the flood wave charging downriver. All I could think of was to blast the truck horn, and try to warn people. I never thought you two—' Her voice caught, and I saw she was nearly crying, too.

I tried to stand. My legs buckled and I nearly fell, but Dad had hold of me. 'I should tan your backside,' he went, then ruffled my hair. 'What on earth were you doing down there?'

Tipene croaked something, struggled up until he was sitting on the muddy grass, while Auntie Whina still held him. 'We saw — this.' He fumbled inside his dripping shirt, and drew out the carving.

Silence. Nobody moved; nobody spoke. Even the river's roar seemed to dwindle. Seven pairs of eyes (this place is like the main street in town, I suddenly thought) gazed at the little panel. Pale sunlight gleamed through clouds, and the paua eyes gleamed.

Only then did Finola gasp and my father start murmuring 'Dear God . . . Dear God.' Mum went 'Oh,

Tipene!' Auntie Whina was murmuring in Maori. I knew some of the words: '. . . water . . . our people'.

'It was stuck on the ledge,' I told them. 'The river must have carried it there.'

Tipene's fingers stroked whorls and diamond shapes. '. . . the swamp?' I heard him say.

Grandad Duncan nodded. 'Your Nana and Great-nana said . . . there were stories.' He sighed.

My mother put her arms around me again. I'd stopped crying now, and I hoped nobody would mention it — ever. 'Honestly, Whina — should we kiss these boys, or skin them alive?'

Tipene's mum smiled, touched the greenstone at her throat. 'Both.' She knelt, kissed Tipene gently on the cheek, and I could see him hoping nobody would ever mention that again, either. Dad and Granddad Duncan stood grinning.

Auntie Whina touched the carving once again. 'Nana Ahorangi and the others must be told.' She bent her head, murmured again. I heard 'taonga'. I knew that word, too; felt proud that I did.

'All right, people.' Dad took my arm, nodded at Finola to help Tipene. 'Let's get these two back home and dried out.'

We began moving towards the road and bridge. The Waimoana growled and swept by a couple of yards away, savage and wonderful. I'd always feel different about it now.

My legs trembled. My back and shoulders felt as if someone had run our farm truck over them. I shuddered with cold and exhaustion.

I glanced over at Tipene, stumbling along beside me, with Finola and Grandad Duncan gripping his arms. He looked even worse than I did, but he flicked a feeble grin at me. Auntie Whina walked behind him, holding the little panel in both hands.

We climbed the fence — that is, five of us climbed; Tipene and I were half-lifted over — and reached the bridge. It was less than an hour ago that I'd been standing near here, thinking how I wanted to stay in this valley, make my life here.

It's *life* that's the real treasure. I knew it now. The carving was amazing, and it would be even more amazing if the swamp held others. But the most precious things could be inside you as well as outside.

We started trudging along the wooden deck of the bridge. I lifted my sore, aching head again, and gazed around. I'd never felt so happy and hopeful in my life.

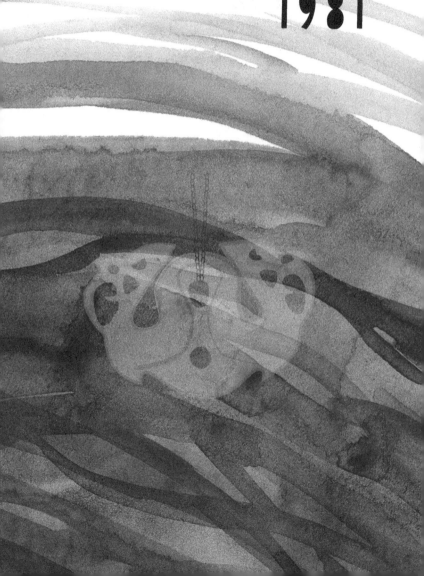

I'm only fourteen, but I'm going to the Auckland march. Mum and Dad weren't too keen, but Nana Florence said: 'We'll make sure she doesn't get into trouble. We girls can do anything, right, Ailsa?'

Nana Whina — she's Dad's friend Tipene's mother; everyone knows everyone else in the Waimoana Valley — said 'Dead right they can.' So Mum laughed and went 'I'm not going to try arguing with you two.'

Dad grinned. 'And I'm not going to try arguing with you *three*.' Even my big bro John laughed, in spite of all the arguments he's been having with everyone.

Then Grandad Matiu went: 'After all, Alan and Beth, just think of the name you gave this girl.'

I'm Ailsa Hahona Hohepa, which I think sounds great, even if a couple of kids at school reckoned Maori and English names don't go together.

Ailsa is Scottish, and means 'victory of the gods'. Amazing, eh? One side of our family came here from Scotland almost a hundred years ago, because they wanted a better life. Dad's part-Scottish and a little bit Maori. Hahona means 'healer', and it's one of Nana

Florence's names, too. A girl called Hahona was the best friend of Nana Florence's nana when she first arrived. My nana's nana (hope you're keeping up!) was called Aggie, and was blind. She and Hahona went everywhere together, Nana Florence says. So that's why I've got my second name.

Anyway, I'm going to Auckland with the others, to march against the Springbok rugby tour.

I love rugby. John used to let me play with him and his friends when we were all little, and I reckon it's rotten that girls can't play it at high school. Dad agrees with me. (He was my primary-school teacher as well as my father, which is so weird. I'll tell you more about that later.) John says if I play, the boys might be embarrassed. That's their problem!

The Springboks are touring New Zealand, and the final test is in Auckland. The All Blacks won the first (yay!); South Africa won the second (boo!). The third game is going to be so important.

But although I like rugby so much, we shouldn't have invited the Springboks to tour here. In South Africa, black and coloured people still aren't allowed in the same restaurants or on the same buses as white people. It's almost impossible to marry someone who's a different colour. Black leaders have been sent to jail for wanting equal rights. Nearly all our family, except John, agree New Zealand should stop playing the Springboks until they treat black and coloured people better.

There have been protest marches outside most games. The match against Waikato had to be called off, after protestors broke through a fence and got onto the ground. A game in Timaru was cancelled, too.

Other people support the tour. Some of them say sport shouldn't be mixed up with politics. Some reckon we should invite the South Africans here so they can see how New Zealanders get along together.

There've been arguments in the paper, on radio and TV. Not just arguments: fights between marchers and rugby fans. When the Waikato game was stopped, the television showed bottles being chucked at the protestors; guys kicking and punching one another. One woman had blood pouring down her face where something had hit her. Mum and Nana Florence were crying as they watched. Even John went silent. I felt sick. And I made my mind up I was going to do something. That's why I'm going to Auckland.

John says the Springboks have got a black player in their team. 'Yeah,' I went. 'One!' He glared at me. Luckily, he works on a couple of farms down the valley, so he's not home very often to have rows.

I'm a bit scared about what might happen at the third test, but I'm excited, too. Some of the kids in my Form Four class at high school wish they were coming; others reckon I'm stupid. The tour has really divided people. There's families in the Waimoana Valley who've stopped speaking to one another.

Dad says there are black rugby organisations in South Africa working to get into the top teams. (He knows those sorts of things. Teachers usually do.) It was embarrassing sometimes, being in his class at primary school, or seeing his name on my report: *Alan Hohepa, Teacher*. But he made lessons interesting.

Mum's a teacher, too; she met my father at teachers' college. She comes from a part of New Zealand where my Great-great-great-Aunt Janet used to live. So when Dad went to teachers' college, he was supposed to say 'hello' to this girl called Beth. He reckons he wasn't very interested — until he met her. She helps teach Standards One and Two at Waimoana School.

I felt nervous during the couple of days before we drove to Auckland. Nervous and excited. I was going to show how I felt about this tour. So I went for walks down the riverbed, past the old orchard and the new bridge that crosses the Waimoana where the swing-bridge used to be. There's no other girls in the valley my age. Dad's friend Tipene and his wife, Pania, (she's neither pro- nor anti-tour) have eleven-year-old twins, Marika and Marama. But I quite like being by myself.

I like the valley, too. I know it's special. Tipene's father, Robert McDougall (I call him Grandad Robert), used to teach at our primary school, and he's writing a book about the Waimoana area. He's found out all sorts of stuff. But I'm going to leave here sometime. There's a big wide world out there, and I want to see it!

The road past our place is tar-sealed now. There are new big milk-tankers that pick up from the farms. We've got TV — though not colour. But it's still a sleepy place, most of the time. I want some excitement in my life.

Some people like living in the Waimoana Valley because it's peaceful. A family from South Vietnam came here about the time I was born. There'd been a long war in their country — even New Zealand soldiers were fighting there for a while — and they arrived in our country as refugees.

I didn't know that Tranh — he's about my age — was from Vietnam when I first met him. 'Is New Zealand very different from China?' I asked him. Tranh got quite wild. 'We not China! We from Vietnam!' His family used to be farmers, and they've started this huge market garden, with all sorts of vegetables.

Tranh comes on the bus to high school. When we were at primary school, he used to do this little bow whenever he saw me, which was embarrassing, but quite cute. He doesn't do it now that he's become a typical rude Kiwi guy! But he wished me good luck when I said why I was going to Auckland.

The day before we left, I walked a long way up and down the riverbed. The Waimoana had a huge flood a long time ago; Dad and Tipene nearly got drowned being silly. For ages after, the river flowed up against the other bank.

It was amazing, their finding that carved panel. It's famous: Grandad Robert has lots of articles from newspapers and magazines about it. It's kept in the meeting house on the marae. I like looking at it whenever we go there.

One article has a photo of Dad and Tipene and Tipene's sister, Finola, holding the panel. 'Stupid boys!' Nana Florence said once. 'They're lucky they didn't end up in the river.'

They made up for it later. The new bridge I was walking under yesterday had to be built because of what happened to the old swing one.

I was about six. My father and Tipene were sorting out our hayshed one morning soon after Christmas. I was 'helping' Mum in the kitchen — getting in her way, in other words. We'd picked a whole bucket of peas from our garden, and we were going to take some over to Nana Florence and Grandad Matiu, in their little cottage just across the road.

I heard a truck start rumbling across the bridge, but I didn't take any notice. After Christmas is when most farmers cut hay for their cows' winter feed, and trucks are always carting bales from one place to another.

Then a different noise made Mum and me freeze. A *bang!*, followed straightaway by a cracking and splintering. Silence for half a second, then the walloping sound of something heavy hitting water.

Mum raced out of the house towards the back path and our home paddock. I tore after her, as fast as my six-year-old legs could carry me. As I pushed through the gate into the paddock, she was already halfway over the stile onto the road. Dad and Tipene were ahead of her, sprinting towards the bridge.

I struggled over the stile and started along the road. I heard myself making little whimpering noises. Something terrible had happened; I just knew it.

I could see the bridge just ahead. Something was different. What . . . then I stopped and stared.

A long chunk of the wooden deck had vanished. I was gazing down through empty air at the stones of the riverbed way below. Up against its steep bank, the Waimoana swept by, deep and powerful. I glimpsed something under the surface. Something red and crumpled-looking. A truck.

Voices shouted. Hands grabbed me. 'Ailsa! Stay here!' My mother pulled me against her. We stood, staring at the twisted shape in the surging river. Where was the driver?

Dad and Tipene had scrambled halfway down the

bank. Another truck skidded to a stop at the far end, figures jumping out. My father and his friend were pulling off boots, stripping off shirts. No movement inside the truck.

My father crouched, facing the river. 'Alan!' Mum called. 'Be careful!' But Dad was already plunging into the water. Tipene leaped, too, straight after him. They disappeared under the surface. I could just make out their shapes, heaving at the door of the crumpled cab. Mum squeezed me against her so hard I thought she was going to squash me.

Tipene and Dad burst up from the water together. They sucked in huge breaths and dived once more. Mum and I stood staring into the river, where the two figures struggled at the truck's door. Brakes squealed behind us, and Mr Ross from up the valley jumped out of his car. He wore his going-to-town clothes: good trousers, shirt and tie.

He hurried up to my mother and me. 'What's happened, Beth? Who is it?'

Mum opened her mouth to speak, then stopped. At the same moment, I saw a different movement under the water. The cab door sagged open; my father half-disappeared inside. Another second, then he and Tipene were dragging someone out into the current.

They shot up to the surface again, clutching the driver between them. Once more I heard them gasping for breath, then they began kicking towards the bank, pulling a limp body with them, trying to keep its head above water.

Mr Ross went sliding down the steep slope. Mrs Ross will be annoyed if he gets his good clothes dirty, I thought — like an idiot.

He seized my father's hand and the driver's shirt; yanked them upwards. Tipene shoved from behind. They struggled up out of the river, and flopped on a level part of the bank.

Dad knelt by the driver, gasping and shaking. Mr Ross and Tipene crouched beside him. After a couple of seconds, Mr Ross raised his head (his going-to-town shirt was filthy; Mrs Ross would be *really* annoyed). 'He's alive!' he called up to Mum and me.

Another car had arrived, too. Nana Florence and Grandad Matiu with Nana Whina. 'Still getting into trouble at the river, you two?' Nana Whina shouted down the bank. 'Don't you ever learn?'

Tipene and my father looked up together. Under their sodden hair, their faces split into grins. 'Sorry, Mum,' Tipene went. 'But this time we're the good guys!'

They got their photos in the paper. The truck driver got out of hospital with a broken wrist a couple of days later. And our valley got a new bridge.

So I was thinking about all that, the day I wandered along the riverbed. About fifty metres past the bridge, someone called to me. No, it was magpies, warbling and squawking in the old orchard. The trees don't give much fruit now, though Nana Florence reckons the plums taste better than ones from the town supermarket. The old orchard is where she and Nana Whina were when the big earthquake struck. There's been some scary stuff happened in our valley!

I don't go to the orchard much. Once when I was nine or so, Mum and Dad and John and I were all there, getting pears for stewing. A couple of magpies started dive-bombing us, swooping and shrieking. One whacked my head with its wing as it skimmed past, and I got a real fright. Dad said they must have a nest nearby. Either that, or they were trying to snatch the butterfly clip in my hair.

About a year after they found the carving and nearly drowned, Dad and Tipene were down on the riverbed near the orchard and saw something glittering among the stones. It was a little round piece of paua shell. Paua, miles from the sea? They took it to Grandad Matiu; he used to study old history and stuff like that. He thought it must be from another carving, maybe washed out of the swamp by the same flood that carried away the carved panel. It's kept on the marae, along with the panel. Nana Whina's mother Ahorangi said prayers in the meeting house over the new find.

She — Ahorangi — is buried at the urupa, near the marae. There's a little memorial to her on the grave of my great-grandparents Duncan and Lily, up in the old part of our cemetery; they were best friends. Yeah, maybe South African people could learn from seeing how our Maori and Pakeha people get along? But the tour is wrong; I still believe that.

I know all the people in our cemetery's new part. In the old part, there are some names that don't live in the valley any more — Smale, Sheffield (though Great-nana Lily was a Sheffield before she married Great-grandad Duncan). I guess people gradually get forgotten after they die. Grandad Robert says that's one reason he's writing his history, to save as many memories as possible. I suppose people will forget me when I'm dead, though that's hard to believe. It's even harder to believe I'll ever die!

As I finally came across the bridge and back into our home paddock, I could hear loud voices. I sighed. My brother John was back and having another argument.

No, he wasn't. He stood on the front verandah of our farmhouse, calling across the road to my father, who was helping Grandad Matiu prop up the branches of the peach trees they've planted beside the cottage. 'Cup of tea, Dad! And Nana and Grandad, if they want.'

Grandad called out that they were just off to visit Nana Whina. They're all helping Grandad Robert McDougall work on his history. (I think they like remembering the old stories together.) Dad said he'd be a minute. Have you noticed that for men 'a minute' usually means quarter of an hour?

John saw me, went 'Hi, Shorty'. I usually get annoyed when he calls me that, but there've been too many rows in our family these past weeks, so I just said 'Hi'.

'Thought I'd better make sure you've got yourselves organised before you head off to be silly sods in Auckland,' my big brother went next. Now my face started to get hot. We didn't need smart comments from him. I opened my mouth to tell him so.

Mum spoke first. 'Thanks, love. Dad says you'll drop in and do the milking while we're away. That's great.' She shot me a quick look, and I knew she was telling me to stay quiet. 'Dad moved the cows down to the river paddock this morning, so there should be plenty of feed.'

John nodded. 'Not a problem.' He glanced at me and said 'Look after your mum and dad and the others, OK?' Suddenly, I realised he was worried about us. For

a moment I felt nervous; then I felt glad he trusted me
— sort of.

'I will,' I told him. 'Thanks for coming.'

John shrugged. 'No big deal. Gotta go, Mum. Can
I take a couple of scones with me?' Next minute, my
mother had four buttered-and-jammed scones in a bag
for him. He left just as Dad appeared: 'a minute' had
meant only five minutes today.

'OK?' my father asked, as soon as he came in. Mum
nodded. 'OK.' I glimpsed the relief on their faces. Yeah,
must be hard for them to have their family split over
the tour.

The next day, we drove up to Auckland. Two carloads
of us: me, Mum and Dad, Nana Florence and Grandad
Matiu, Uncle Tipene and Nana Whina. Auntie Pania
hugged Tipene hard before he left. 'Be sensible! I know
what you and Alan are like when you get together.'

Tipene grinned. The scar on his forehead, where
he'd bashed it when he and Dad were stuck in the
Waimoana, wrinkled like it often does. 'No rivers at
the rugby ground, honey.'

Pania snorted. 'You two can find trouble whether it's
wet or dry!' She looked at me. 'You stay out of trouble,
too. Don't go beating up any Springboks!'

Nana Whina kissed Auntie Pania and the twins. 'Can't we go, too?' Marama asked. 'Yeah, can't we?' echoed Marika.

Nana Whina laughed. 'Someone has to keep an eye on your Grandad Robert. You two make sure he behaves himself.' The girls looked pleased.

Great-uncle Robert McDougall wanted to come with us, but someone needed to be at home just in case anything happened. So he'd agreed to stay.

Nana Whina wore the little greenstone bat around her neck. I glanced at Nana Florence and stared. The silver bracelet wasn't on her wrist. Then I saw its plaited band and thistle clasp glinting on my mother's. So it was her turn to wear it now. Someday it would be mine. I didn't want to think about that; it would mean Mum was getting old.

We climbed into the cars, waved goodbye to Auntie Pania and the twins, and headed off down the valley for Auckland and the third rugby test.

Three kilometres along the road, a farm truck was parked in a driveway. A figure stood beside it, watching us come. John.

We slowed down. My brother gazed at us, shook his head, then called out. I heard '. . . careful . . . safe'.

We waved again, drove on again. My parents smiled at each other, and I felt better, too.

We had a good time driving up. Mum and Dad checked out all the farms we passed. 'Nice-looking heifers,' I heard. 'Fencing must have cost a packet . . . paddocks looking heavy.' When we drove through a town, Dad looked bored; Mum tried to see into the shop windows. As soon as I can, I'm going to live in a place with lots of people and lots of things happening.

A train rumbled across a bridge on our left. My father murmured: 'Mum still can't bear to look at anything like that.' I knew he was talking about how Great-uncle Angus died. I glanced through our car's back window, at Matiu's green car with Nana Florence, Nana Whina and Tipene, but I couldn't make out their faces.

Nana told me once how a special funeral service was held for Great-uncle Angus on the Waimoana Marae — the 'pa', people used to call it — because we've always had so many friends there. I want to make them proud of me, I suddenly thought. I'm going to be careful, but I want my own family and my friends' families to feel I've done something good up in Auckland.

Some of our cousins' cousins' cousins, or something like that, live a couple of hours' drive from us. One of them brought his bagpipes across to my great-uncle's funeral, to play a farewell. As soon as Ahorangi and the other old Maori people saw them, they started chuckling. Their ancestors thought the pipes were a monster shrieking. I don't blame them!

A few of those Scottish rellies are driving up to the Auckland protest, too. Maybe we'll see them. I've got a cousin — all right, a cousin's cousin's etc — about my age. I met him once; he was skinny and pretty boring.

Our Waimoana Marae is quite famous. Like I said, the panel Dad and Tipene found is kept there, and people come to learn carving and weaving and stuff. Tipene is a really good carver. He did this incredible thing with the walking stick that Great-grandad Duncan used, and that's on the wall of my grandparents' cottage.

The stick used to be the handle of Duncan's axe. It helped save him after he hurt himself really badly, and Nana Florence says it saved Dad and Tipene when they got stuck in the flood that time. After he began carving, Tipene 'borrowed' the stick, carved it with patterns like the ones from the panel they'd found, and gave it back to our family.

There could be other things in the swamp. After Dad and Tipene found the panel, there was a lot of talk on the marae about whether to search for more. A university group got permission to dig in one part, near the river, where the panel might have come from. They didn't find anything, and people decided they didn't want our valley's special place dug up any more.

★

We reached the motor camp about three o'clock. We weren't staying in a tent: Dad had booked us a couple of cabins. I felt quite excited; I'd never slept in a cabin before.

The manager or whoever looked at us when we trooped into the office. 'You people going on that protest nonsense?'

I saw Tipene frown and my father glare. My face went hot, and I opened my mouth. But it was Mum who spoke first. 'Protest, yes. Nonsense, no. Looks like you're nice and full. What a pretty campground.'

My clever mother! No wonder she's a good teacher. You could tell that the manager didn't know what to do. He shuffled some papers. 'There's a twenty-dollar damage and good behaviour bond for every person.'

'You didn't mention that when I phoned.' Dad's voice was tight.

'Yeah, well I've got to think about—'

'Are you charging tour supporters twenty dollars as well?' Nana Whina spoke quietly.

The guy's face went red. 'That's my business.'

'It's *our* business.' Nana Whina still didn't raise her voice. 'Are you telling me that one group of New Zealanders don't have the rights of another group?'

Now Nana Florence cut in. This was starting to sound like a school debate. 'As my daughter-in-law says, you've got a nice place here. We'll respect it. We're going on the march because we believe people *deserve* respect. I'm sure you feel the same way.'

The guy tossed two keys on the counter. 'Don't use all the hot water in the shower blocks, eh? There's other people to think of.'

Mum gave him a dazzling smile. 'That's exactly why we're marching: to think of other people. Thank you so much.'

Dad and Tipene looked as if they wanted to say something else, but Nana Florence and my mother eased us outside. 'What a lovely man!' Mum grinned, when we were on our way back to the cars.

'Huh,' grunted Tipene. 'I'd like to—'

'"Lovely?"' muttered Dad at the same time. 'I wanted to—' He and Tipene stopped, stared at each other, began to laugh.

A voice called 'Hello! You're here! Kia ora — welcome!'

It was Finola, Tipene's elder sister. She lives in Auckland and teaches at the university. 'Big sis got all the brains and I got all the good looks,' Tipene smirked when she was down visiting one time. Finola laughed. 'You're half-right. I won't say which half . . .'

Finola's writing a book, too. Hers is about Maori women: the things they've done; the ways they're the guardians of songs and stories. She comes to Waimoana to do research a lot; reckons she's going to steal Grandad Robert's best stories and put them in *her* book.

She told me one time about some of the women from Waimoana Marae. Areta, who came to the valley with her people when a war drove them off their lands, and who tried to heal Great-great-nana Aggie's blindness. Her daughter Hahona, who became Aggie's best friend. Hahona's young sister, Ngaio, who married one of our family and taught kids at our very first school how to speak Maori.

Finola met my Great-great-aunt Jess (yeah, so many 'greats') when Jess was old. She lived in Auckland, too, and was really famous for campaigning about women's rights and stuff like that. 'It's not just now that girls can do anything, Ailsa,' Finola told me once. 'Girls and women have *always* been able to do anything.'

Finola had rung Tipene a few days back to say she was coming on the march. 'Not in the Patu Squad. I'll go on the main march with you lot. You'll get lost otherwise.'

The Patu Squad is mainly young protestors. ('Patu' is a type of club used by Maori warriors in the old times.) They've marched and demonstrated at a lot of games. Most of them wear motorbike helmets, and pad their jackets with cardboard and things like that, because they try to break into the rugby grounds, and sometimes they've ended up in fights with police or tour supporters. I said once at home how it must be exciting to do something like that, how I'd like to— Dad stuck his finger almost in my face and went 'You are *not* joining any Patu Squad!'

In Wellington, a whole crowd of protestors tried to march into the grounds of Parliament Buildings. The police stopped them. There was shoving and punching, and the TV showed women crying, a man staggering with a big gash on his forehead, people lying crumpled on the ground. Mum feels sorry for the police; they're just trying to do their jobs. I suppose so, but if anyone tries to shove me . . .

We unloaded our stuff into the cabins. I grabbed the top bunk. (Actually, Mum and Dad told me they were grabbing the bottom bunks.) We piled into our car and Finola's car, and she took us all to a fish-and-chip shop a couple of kilometres away. It was crowded, too. A bunch of guys about John's age watched us come in. They looked like rugby supporters (don't ask me why I thought that), and you could tell they were wondering if we were anti-tour weirdoes. But Mum and Nana Florence started yakking to them, and one of them turned out to have an uncle just a couple of valleys away from Waimoana. We all said 'See you' and 'Good luck' to one another when we left, though I didn't feel sure what their idea of good luck might be.

I climbed up into my bunk pretty early that night. Funny how sitting in a car seat for half a day makes you feel tired.

I heard Finola saying how there was barbed wire all around Eden Park, where the third test was going to be played, and rows of those huge steel rubbish skips were being lined up along some roads near the ground to stop anyone breaking through. Sounds like a war zone, I thought as I slid off to sleep. In some ways our little country was exactly that, as long as the tour lasted.

I felt churned-up at breakfast next morning. We'd brought eggs and stuff from the farm. (Real country people, eh?) 'Big breakfast for a big day, love,' Mum went as she and Nana Florence and Nana Whina cooked, and all eight of us somehow squeezed in around the table. But her face looked serious, and only a few people grinned.

'All right, everyone,' Grandad Matiu went when we'd finished eating. 'We oldies have been talking about what we're going to do. Everyone ready to hear their orders?'

We were going to leave the campground about ten o'clock. The game didn't start until three, but Finola said the marchers would be forming up in their squads earlier. She'd meet us at a street a couple of kilometres away. 'Best to park your cars where they're safe,' she told the others. I knew what she meant: after the game against Waikato was stopped by those protestors getting onto the field, some angry rugby fans smashed up cars that had *STOP THE TOUR* stickers.

We were going to march with the groups that didn't intend to try and climb over fences or skips or anything. 'We'll only make the tour supporters angrier,' Tipene said, and heads nodded. 'Anyway,' grinned Grandad Matiu, 'it's all I can do to climb over the stile at home these days.' We'd do whatever the police told us to; stay polite. If any pro-tour people started an argument with us, we'd tell them how we all loved rugby (true!), but we wanted to show how we felt apartheid was wrong.

'And I'll tell them to be kind to an old bloke,' went Mum. 'Your father, I mean, Ailsa.' Dad tried to look insulted.

We didn't have any motorbike helmets, but we all wore thick jackets. 'Even demonstrators can catch a cold,' Nana Florence said.

Mum was undoing the gleaming silver bracelet from around her wrist. 'Don't want to lose this. Besides, if anyone grabs me, it could give a nasty cut.' She looked across at me. 'Here, Ailsa, love. You keep it in your pocket for me.'

Another hand reached out. Nana Whina held her

glowing little pounamu bat. 'Take this too, dear. They'll both look after you. They'll give you strength.'

I mumbled 'Thanks', or something stupid. I carefully folded up the bracelet and necklace, and pushed them deep into a front pocket of my jeans. I felt . . . special. Yeah, I thought again; I'm going to make them proud of me.

Nana Florence stood. 'Right, I'm going to make a nice big thermos of tea to take with us.' I couldn't help grinning. Going on a protest march past cops, barbed wire, and edgy rugby fans with a nice thermos of tea. How hilarious.

Groups of people were moving out of the campground. A couple of women about the same age as my nanas were carrying signs: *HALT ALL RACIST TOURS* and *FREEDOM FOR BLACK PEOPLE*. Three young guys in what looked like rugby scarves started laughing. 'Reckon you'll do any good, grandma?' one called out to the women.

'More than you are,' I heard myself go. 'Why don't you stick up for black people?' The rugby guys said nothing; walked on. Mum shook her head at me.

The campground manager stood on the porch of his office, arms folded, staring at us as we drove off. Nana Florence and I waved to him; he didn't wave back.

★

We found the side street Finola had mentioned. It was full of wooden houses with corrugated-iron roofs, just like our place back home, except the lawns were so small, not even a calf could have found enough to eat. Wonder if I'll ever live in a place like this? I thought.

Finola was waiting for us. So were a man and a teenage boy. Mum exclaimed as we got out of our car; hugged the man and then the boy, who gave an embarrassed grin. He'd been staring at me until I stared at him; then we both looked away.

'You remember Uncle Mac, Ailsa?' Mum said to me. 'And Robbie.' Of course: my skinny, boring sort-of-cousin. Except he was taller and stronger-looking now.

We locked the cars, and Dad patted the bonnet of ours. 'See you later,' he told it. We zipped up our jackets, Tipene took the bag with our thermos of tea (shame!), and we started off, following Finola.

People streamed along the footpath. Some carried signs: protest supporters. Some carried rugs and cushions: tour supporters. The different groups looked hard at one another as they walked. There was a bit of muttering, but nothing more. Uncle Mac walked ahead, with Dad and Tipene. Not-so-skinny Robbie was behind me, while Nana Florence asked him all about what was happening to every rellie in his part of the world, poor guy. His voice sounded deeper than last time.

We turned down another street. The crowd grew thicker as we walked. I glimpsed a line of blue along one footpath. Police, in helmets and plastic face-visors, standing with hands behind backs, watching everyone who passed. From their belts hung batons nearly as long as my arm. I'd heard about those from the TV news; they were for jabbing people in the ribs if they didn't move, whacking their hands and heads if a fight started. I decided I'd stay *very* polite, like Grandad Matiu had told me. There were about twelve police, plus some clowns and a bumble-bee.

Bumble-bee? I gaped. A girl, about eighteen or nineteen, wearing a striped black-and-yellow costume. She stood at one end of the police line, hands behind her back, too, a serious expression on her face, just like the police. She saw me staring, and winked.

The policeman next to her glanced down, made like he'd just noticed her, snapped to attention, and threw her a salute. The bumble-bee girl put two black-and-yellow arms around his waist and snuggled up. The crowd laughed; some clapped. I felt myself relax.

'Good, eh?' The throng of people had brought us to a stop, and Robbie was beside me. Suddenly I felt pleased I'd worn my new jeans. I mumbled something.

'The main march is gonna come past here,' Finola announced. 'How about we wait and join it then?' We leaned against a brick front wall, while others poured by. A couple of hundred metres away, at the end of the road, square shapes gleamed in the low winter sun. The steel rubbish skips, as big as garden sheds. Barbed wire lay coiled in front of them. Police and guys in white coats were checking tickets before they let anyone through.

'See that?' Robbie pointed at the next wall along. A garden gnome sat on it. No, a concrete frog, holding a sign. We eased through the crowd to read it: *DON'T SIT ON THE FENCE. STOP THE TOUR.*

We both laughed. 'You been on any other marches?' my something-cousin asked.

'No, just this one. You?'

'Went on one through town a couple of weeks back. Only about twenty of us. There was this woman on the footpath watching us — looked a bit like my mum. She called out "Stupid fools! You deserve a good kick!" So Dad went: "You mean like black people get in South Africa?"'

I laughed again. Then I realised Robbie had gone silent. A bunch of young guys with *STAND UP FOR RUGBY* badges on their jackets had stopped nearby. They'd been watching us as we'd laughed at the frog and its sign. Now one of them said something to his mates, and they started towards us. My stomach lurched. I felt my fists clench. Mum and Dad and the others were about twenty metres away. They hadn't noticed.

Robbie spoke loudly. 'The All Black forwards are better than theirs, eh? But we'll have to watch those Springbok backs.'

What was he—? Then I understood, and replied 'Yeah. We gotta keep the game tight, eh?' The rugby guys walked off. Robbie and I both went 'Whew!' and laughed — quietly.

★

'Better not lose the others,' I said, and we moved back towards where the rest of our group stood. Grandad Matiu smiled at us. 'Thought you'd gone sightseeing.'

Time passed. More rugby fans filtered through the line of white coats up ahead. Couldn't be long until the game started now. I wouldn't mind a cup of Nana Florence's tea. I yawned. A small plane droned overhead, began a slow circle. TV or something? Yeah, just as well I'd worn my good jeans.

More time dragged by. Then my head jerked up as a different sound grew at the end of the street we'd come down. Tramping feet. More police? A whole team of rugby fans? Then I saw the signs and motorbike helmets swing around the corner, and heard the chanting.

They marched with arms linked, eight or ten abreast. Would we be doing that, too, in the main march? Some wore balaclavas, covering their faces except for eyeholes. One sign read *PATU;* others *STOP THE TOUR* and *FREEDOM FOR ALL RACES* . . . Their ranks tramped by, a hundred of them maybe, heading towards the skips and barbed wire. They looked fierce and determined, and for a few seconds, I wished I was one of them. I let out the breath I'd been holding.

More feet were approaching, but not tramping like the Patu Squad. Signs, but no helmets. Men and women, dark heads, fair heads, grey heads, even a few bald heads. A contingent of nuns, and even a priest carrying a large crucifix. The main march. My heart began to beat faster.

Dad raised his voice. 'This is us, people. Stay safe, remember. If we get separated, meet back at the car.'

Some people on the footpath were clapping. A few called 'Useless!' 'Get a proper job!' 'Grow up!' The last lines of marchers had almost reached us. An old guy with a walking stick hobbled along. Two girls about my age — grandchildren? — were with him, chanting 'Freedom! Stop the tour! Freedom!' A huge excitement rose up inside me. I'd remember today for the rest of my life. We stepped off the footpath, and joined the other protestors.

Nana Florence and Mum held hands. Finola and Nana Whina were doing the same. Dad, Uncle Tipene and Grandad Matiu squared their shoulders. Uncle Mac put an arm around Robbie for a second, and I knew he was proud of his son. My own parents were going to feel proud of me.

We didn't get very far. Up ahead, by the bins and barbed wire, the Patu Squad stood eyeball-to-eyeball with the police, stamping and chanting. 'One, two, three, four! We don't want this racist tour! Freedom! Freedom!' The police didn't move.

Our march slowed to a halt, a few yards behind. I realised that Dad was gripping one of my arms, Uncle Tipene the other. Uncle Mac and my almost-cousin were just ahead of us. The people around us started chanting, too. 'One, two, three, four! We don't want—' Next minute, I was yelling along with them. Voices I recognised joined in: Mum and Nana Florence. A TV crew appeared, squeezing along the footpath. I thought of the Waimoana Valley, our farm, the marae and the people maybe watching at this moment. I lifted my head, and chanted louder.

The small plane appeared again, circled once more: really low this time. Maybe Auntie Pania and Grandad Robert would be seeing us from above as well. I could just imagine John shaking his head.

A different shout from behind the skips up ahead. A cheer, inside Eden Park itself. The third test must have started. Hope we win, I thought. Our non-marching march chanted louder, and I felt relieved I hadn't thought out loud.

★

Ten minutes passed. It was cold, standing still. I shoved hands in pockets, felt my fingers touch the bracelet and little pounamu bat.

Pushing and shoving began somewhere in front of us. The front ranks of the Patu Squad were trying to force their way towards the park gates. A voice barked orders over a megaphone. More blue uniforms hurried out from behind the bins, and pushed back.

Another ten or fifteen minutes crawled by. I was getting hoarse from chanting. Robbie turned around to look behind him, caught my eye and grinned.

A drone swelled to a roar. The plane flashed past above us, so low that people cried out. It skimmed the top of Eden Park's main grandstand. A scatter of white squares fluttered down. 'Leaflets!' Tipene shouted. 'He's a demonstrator! He's on our side!'

More cheers and yells from around us. Signs waved; faces squinted up. The police watched, too, while the plane dipped and climbed over the grandstands. Then another, louder cheer, from inside the park. 'The All Blacks must have scored,' Robbie went. I nodded. 'Hope so.' We both glanced around in a guilty sort of way.

Again the plane dived. Something else fell from it: something small but solid-looking. It plunged down and vanished. 'What's that?' Mum went.

Another dive. Two more shapes plummeted down. One smacked onto the grandstand roof. An explosion of white rose and hung in the air. 'Flour bombs!' Uncle Mac exclaimed. 'The cheeky sod's dropping flour bombs!'

We laughed and clapped. The rows of marchers were edging forward, trying to get a better view of what was happening. Up ahead, by the skips and barbed wire, signs waved and fists pumped the air. The Patu Squad's crash helmets surged at the blue lines of police. A wooden shield sent a blue helmet flying. The megaphone snapped more orders.

At the front, bodies from both sides suddenly charged hard together. Invisible hands seemed to clutch the two sides and sweep them against each other. The Patu Squad lunged forward; the police flung them back. Long batons jabbed and swung. A crash helmet skittered along the ground. Someone in a blue jacket doubled over and sagged to their knees.

'Oh, be careful!' Nana Florence gasped. She and Mum grasped at each other. Finola gripped Nana Whina's hand.

A figure in the Patu Squad lifted their sign and swung it at the police officer opposite. More wooden shields barged forward. Next second, batons were crashing down on them. A hand held my arm: Robbie, straining to see what was happening among the milling figures ahead.

Around the huge rubbish skips, in front of the barbed wire, arms flailed and bodies rammed into one another. A stick or something whacked into a policeman's side, and he reeled away, clutching at his ribs. The plane snarled overhead; another load of flour bombs and then flares plunged down onto the invisible playing field.

Dad and Tipene had their arms around the two Nanas. Uncle Mac and Grandad Matiu were talking urgently to each other, peering back the way we'd come.

A surge heaved through the whole crowd of demonstrators. Bodies lurched, cannoned into others. Figures fell, dragging others down with them. People nearby tried to keep clear; some of them tripped and toppled over as well. Shouts and screams rang out. I was flung up against Robbie, and the breath whooshed out of me. My part-cousin held me harder. My heart was thumping.

Another surge. More yelling and screaming. Robbie and I collided with his father; grabbed at him. I glimpsed police batons swinging. Fence pickets and signs cracked down at the blue uniforms.

An even fiercer heave drove through the crowd. Helmets barged towards us — crash helmets, police helmets, figures underneath them wrestling and scrambling. Faces shouted and snarled. Mouths gaped open in fear.

Somebody's shoulder slammed into me, and I sprawled sideways. Robbie's hand slipped from my arm. Next minute, I was on the ground. I heard myself wail 'No! Please!' All around me, kicks and punches flew. Someone's knee smacked against my side as I crouched, and I cried out.

Another figure landed beside me. Dad. He wrapped his arms around me, and clasped me to him while people stumbled past. 'Up!' he grunted. 'Can you?' He began struggling to his feet, yanking at my jacket. Another hand pulled at my shoulder: a woman I'd never seen before, hair all over her face. Then I was standing, clutched in my father's grip, shaking and sobbing.

The men got us away. I hate to admit it, but this was one time girls couldn't do everything. They held our arms, gripped our hands, and slowly we started pushing back through the jostling, shouting ranks behind us. Others were leaving as well. There were white, shocked faces; angry faces; weeping faces. Ordinary people who'd never been in anything like this before. And I was one of them.

Dad clutched Mum's elbow. Uncle Mac grasped mine. We picked our way among the cram of figures. A girl a few years older than me sat on the ground sobbing, while two others bent over her.

Chanting started again, back behind us. *'Move! Move! Move!'* Grandad Matiu grunted 'Watch out, everyone!' I snatched a look back, and a double line of police were advancing from the rubbish skips into the protestors. *'Move! Move!'* Long batons jabbed at anyone in their way.

We kept retreating, as fast as we could. The road and footpath were strewn with broken signs, jackets, a couple of crash helmets. By a lamp-post, as we hurried past, a guy in white overalls, with an arm-band reading *Apartheid Sucks*, was dabbing at the forehead of someone in a black and yellow jacket. He reached down into a First Aid box on the ground beside him, pulled out a bandage.

I jerked to a halt. 'Come on, Ailsa, love!' Dad urged. 'Keep moving!' But I was staring at the weeping figure on whose blood-smeared head the First Aid guy was now fixing the bandage. It was the bumble-bee girl I'd seen hugging and smiling at the policeman, two hours ago.

The crowd was starting to thin out. A few stood holding signs, gazing back towards the park where the chant of *'Move! Move!'* still rose, while yells and cries sounded around it. But most people were heading away, like us. A couple nursed hurt arms; another was limping. One man shouted 'Bloody rugby thugs!'

In the houses on either side of the road, people stood

at gates or on verandahs, while the crowd hurried or stumbled past. A middle-aged woman ahead of us sat down suddenly on the low wall she was passing, put her head in her hands, and burst into tears. 'Serves you right!' a man on the garden path inside the wall went. 'Sticking your nose into other people's business!'

I glared at him, tried to think of something to say. Nana Whina and Finola moved over to the crying woman. Nana Whina took her hand; Finola sat on the wall beside her.

'Get going!' the guy yelled. 'I'm not having trouble-makers here!'

'You stupid—' I began. But Mum interrupted me. 'In that case, *you'd* better stop making trouble.' She stood gazing at the man. 'This lady's upset, and maybe hurt. Perhaps you'd like to help her?'

The guy took a step forward, then stopped. 'I'm going to ring the cops. They'll sort you bloody rabble out!' He wheeled around, stalked off up the path towards his house.

'I think the police have quite enough to deal with today.' Nana Florence reached inside the bag Tipene was holding, brought something out, and nodded to the crying woman, who'd lifted her head and was trying to smile.

'Here,' went Nana Florence. 'This'll make you feel better.' And towards the woman, she held out a . . . a cup of tea.

Ten minutes later, we were all at the cars. No broken windows or kicked-in doors, thank goodness. My side hurt from where that knee had rammed into me; I kept shaking. The others were unhurt, except for Grandad Matiu, who had a graze along one cheek. 'Woman poked me with her umbrella, when she was pointing at that plane. Took her ten minutes to stop apologising.'

Other cars were pulling out and driving off. 'Better not hang around too long,' Uncle Mac said. 'The game'll be over any minute. Some of the pro-tour lot might be looking for a fight.'

'They'll be in a good mood,' Robbie announced. We stared at him; he looked embarrassed, then pulled a little transistor radio from his jacket pocket. 'Just heard the final score, actually. The All Blacks won.'

He and Uncle Mac were staying over on the far side of Auckland. While the adults said good-bye, he looked at me. 'Might be coming over your way, Dad says. You've got a great-uncle or somebody who's writing a book about your valley? Dad wants to try something like that for our place; he might drive across for a few tips. See you, eh?'

'Yeah,' I went, as we started getting into our cars. 'See you.' I closed the door, gave him a wave, and started trying to work out how I could meet him when he came.

★

We climbed into our bunks early that night. I had a big red patch on my ribs. One of my feet was sore, where somebody must have trodden on it. Nana Whina, Nana Florence and Grandad Matiu looked exhausted. Uncle Tipene kept rubbing the scar on his forehead. We all yawned as we talked.

But I still buzzed with excitement. I'd done something that I'd remember for ever. Other people would remember *me*. I gazed around at my sleepy family and friends, and thought how special they all were.

Dad and Tipene and I went out to buy a Chinese takeaway. While I stood by the car, shivering a bit in the cool evening, I pushed my hands into my jeans pockets; touched the silver bracelet and little greenstone bat tucked away there. I'd offered them back to Nana Whina and Mum when we reached the campground, but Nana Whina smiled and said, 'Keep them until we get home, Ailsa, dear. You've earned them.' I grew ten centimetres taller right then.

When we got back with the takeaways, the campground was quiet, except for people getting into another car a few cabins down. A torch shone on us as we climbed out. 'Make sure there's no noise after ten o'clock,' the camp manager grunted.

'How about snoring?' Dad asked him. 'We allowed to do that?'

The manager shot him a dirty look. 'Didn't do any good this afternoon, did you? Test got played. Cops stopped you rabble from causing trouble.'

I clenched my fists and glared. Then a voice spoke from the car into which people were climbing. 'Leave them alone, mate. They're all right, eh?'

It was the rugby guys, the ones who'd sneered at the woman with her sign, called her 'grandma'. 'They're all right,' the man called again.

'Make sure you leave the place tidy in the morning.' The manager's torch moved off.

'Thanks, mate,' Uncle Tipene called to the figures around the other car. 'Good luck.'

'Cheers,' the reply came back. 'We showed those Springboks, eh?'

Yeah, I thought to myself, as our cabin door opened and Mum asked 'You going to stand out there gossiping all night?' I hope we showed the Springboks lots of things.

I dreamed all sorts of things that night. About the greenstone bat and the little carved panel, and the axe handle stick on Nana Florence's and Grandad Matiu's wall. In one dream, I was walking along the riverbed while magpies dropped bits of paua shell around me. Every time one landed, the ground trembled like there was an earthquake. Another time, I was in the old part of our cemetery, reading the really early names on graves. Helen . . . Niall . . . John . . . Aggie . . . Angus. The Waimoana River had flooded, a really massive torrent of water rushing past the cemetery. But I wasn't scared; I knew I could handle anything.

Anything except for feeling so stiff and creaky. I ached all over. I kept falling asleep on the drive home.

The others were quiet, too. 'Wonder if we'll be on the news?' Uncle Tipene said at breakfast. 'Wonder what happened to that guy in the plane?'

'I hope nobody was badly hurt,' Mum murmured. 'Do you think it was all worth it?'

Nana Florence patted my mother's arm. 'Beth, dear, our family came to New Zealand to find a place where people were treated fairly. We marched because we want people in South Africa to have that, as well.'

I sat there, feeling so good — and so stiff. I touched the bracelet on my wrist and the pendant at my throat. I wore them both all the way home. I wanted to remember everything that had happened in Auckland. I'd have so much to tell Tranh and the other kids on the bus to school. And I'm gonna tell John, too: make my big brother listen. I'm not going to have a fight, but I want to really show him how I feel. And I'll listen to him, too.

Actually (and this is really amazing), John might *read* about me sometime. Finola is going to write a chapter in her book about Maori women who protested against the Springbok Tour, and those who supported them. Be so cool to see my name in a book! Maybe Grandad Robert will put us in his book as well?

I fell asleep in the back seat — again. I woke up when we stopped at a picnic spot to eat the sandwiches Mum and Nana Florence had made in the cabin (the cabin we'd left *very* clean and *very* tidy) before we left. With the sandwiches we had — ta-da! — another cup of thermos tea.

I'd been thinking as we drove. I still want to travel, live in other places, try all sorts of special stuff. In the past couple of days, I've really done things. I've marched, and yelled and sung chants, and stood up for what I believe in. Yeah, and I've fallen over and felt scared. I've met Robbie again, and seen ordinary people behave in ways I never thought they could. You can do anything if you make your mind up. Really original thought, eh?

But I'm glad to be going back to our quiet little valley. This will sound corny, but I reckon that if there actually is any more treasure in Waimoana, it's just being able to live in such a special place. You can have rich things inside you as well as outside. (Dunno if that means anything, but it does to me.) Wonder if anyone's ever thought *that* original and amazing thought before?

MAGGIE
1999

I 'm exhausted. I've just spent an hour showing Mum how to search the World Wide Web.

The Web was invented a few years ago, and it's so brilliant for learning stuff. Mum's always been interested in ideas, so she was keen to get it when the internet came to our part of the valley. But she keeps trying to use the phone while she's on the computer, which you can't do on dial-up, of course. So I've been showing her. Grandad Alan and Nana Beth have tried it, too. Grandad's still teaching at Waimoana School, and he says it could be useful there, 'if computers ever catch on'. But he reckons he's a bit old now to understand all this new stuff.

I love it. I want to be a writer sometime, or maybe a doctor. Computers and the Web are going to be so important for studying. Plus they'll help me, since I can't do some stuff other kids can.

I read books, too. I've even read the history of our valley that Great-great-uncle Robert McDougall wrote, before he died about ten years ago. Some of it's a bit dry, but it's got lots of stories about my family and people around here. I learned heaps!

This morning, I was showing Mum how to look up stuff about Scotland on the Web. Some of our family came from there, about 110 years ago. Incredible, eh? Mum's name — Ailsa — is Scottish. So is mine. I'm Maggie, partly after my Great-great-great-(I think I've got the right number!)-nana Aggie. She sounds amazing; she went blind when she was just a girl, but she could do almost anything, like all girls. Thinking of Aggie makes me feel better about what's happened to me.

My brothers Cameron (older than me, and a big pain), and Sholto (younger than me, and another pain) have Scottish names, too. My dad Robbie's family came from Scotland, too, almost as long ago as Mum's. I've got heaps of cousins on Dad's side, and some of the guys are quite cute. Don't tell anyone I said that.

Dad doesn't live with us now. He and my mother met on a protest march, would you believe! They were demonstrating against the 1981 Springbok rugby tour of New Zealand, because South Africa still had laws segregating black and white people then. Afterwards, they went on heaps of other protests. They demonstrated against nuclear tests and spy bases in New Zealand, in favour of gay rights and Maori land claims. Some people in the valley didn't like it; said they were just stirrers. A few people even reckoned I got sick because Mum used to take me with them, and the stress must have affected me. That's so stupid. It really sucks.

Like I say, Mum's still interested in ideas, and in protest causes. She keeps telling me that you have to *do* something, not just complain. She also reckons women are better at getting a message across. Though Dad says that on some protests, she carried the carved walking stick that was part of Great-great-(pause to count)-grandad Duncan's axe, and she'd wave it in the air, which always made people listen very carefully to her.

There's a story about the stick in Great-etc-uncle Robert's book: how it saved Duncan's life and my Grandad Alan's life, too. I sometimes take it with me when I go for walks, and make up stories to myself about the things it's seen. I guess that's one way writers learn how to write.

Dad and Mum split up about four years after I was born; Mum says they probably married too young. They're still good friends, and he visits us as often as he can. He works for a charity that helps villages in the Pacific Islands get fresh water and things like that. If I become a doctor, I'd like to work in those places.

My parents lived in the city for a while, because Mum wanted to. But sometimes they didn't have enough money to pay the rent, so they came back to Waimoana. I was just a baby; Mum reckons I used to cry all the time in town. As soon as we arrived here, I stopped!

Dad built us a small place just across the road from the farmhouse. The new farmhouse, Nana Beth and Grandad Alan call it; the one before it got wrecked in a big earthquake, about sixty years ago. Uncle John and his family live there now; he's taken over the farm, and he does all sorts of new things with it.

You want to hear something amazing about my Uncle John? He married a friend of Mum's; someone she got to know on protest marches. Auntie Kate says the first few times she met my uncle, she spent all the time arguing with him, because he was pro-Springbok Tour, pro-American nuclear ships — the exact opposite of all the things she and Mum believed in. Auntie Kate reckons the only way she could get my uncle to think sensibly was to marry him.

Anyway, we're just sixty steps from their front gate, and just forty steps from the other cottage, where Nana Beth and Grandad Alan live, along with about twenty fruit trees, now that the ones in the old orchard don't grow much fruit.

Dad wanted to come back and live with us again when I first got sick. But Mum said it was really important for him to keep helping people the way he does. He's tall and strong, and sometimes when he's here, he looks at me like he wants to hug all the disease out of me. But he can't.

★

I've got leukaemia. It's a type of cancer where you don't have enough proper blood cells and too many white ones. You bruise easily, and bleed a lot if you get hurt — sometimes inside your body, which can be pretty dangerous. You're tired a lot, and you catch other sicknesses. You can die from it.

Mine started to show when I was about eight. I had all sorts of aches and pains, and I kept waking up at night, shivering and sweating. I started to get bruises on my legs and front, even though I hadn't really bumped myself. Our doctor in town sent me for blood tests, and they showed what it was.

So I've had lots of treatment. Mostly it's chemo-therapy. I go to the hospital in town every three months or so, and they drip these chemicals into my arm through a tube. They're meant to stop the white blood cells from reproducing too much. I usually feel pretty yucky for a week afterwards, but then I can go back to school. I'm lucky: my hair hasn't fallen out, like some people's does.

Nobody knows for sure what causes leukaemia. Like I say, some people reckon it was because Mum and Dad took me on those marches, where everyone got worked up, and there were cars driving past with their exhaust fumes. But Dr Koen — he's the one who looks after me mainly — reckons that's ignorant nonsense. (He says '*ignahrent nahnsense*' in his South African accent, which sounds cool.)

I have to be careful not to knock myself, because of the bruising and bleeding. So I can't play much sport, which is a pain — yeah, a pain to save me from pain. I'd love to play rugby. There's this brilliant New Zealand women's team called the Black Ferns. They won the Women's Rugby World Cup last year, and I wish I could play for them. Maybe I will: most kids who have leukaemia survive, and I'm gonna be one of them!

Being sick has changed my life. But it's also helped me make up my mind. I'm going to get the very best out of every day. And this might sound weird, but I can do things that other kids can't.

I feel down, sometimes. Once after I'd had my chemo, and spent a week at home feeling grotty (but Mum still made me do my assignments!), I went back to school and the other kids were full of this amazing Outdoor Pursuits Course they'd been on. They were laughing about how Chantelle had fallen off the flying-fox, and the disgusting stuff the boys cooked when it was their turn to do dinner. I sat there, still feeling tired and achy, and I'd have given anything in the world to be like them. Anything.

I'm not lonely, even though I'm off school a fair bit. I've got friends who come to see me. My family are really cool. Even my brothers are pretty good — for boys. But I spend a lot of time by myself, when I'm recovering from chemo, and because, like I said, I can't go out and do some things other kids can. So I've learned to do stuff on my own.

I like going for walks along the riverbed. I get there over the 'new' bridge. It's nearly thirty years old; that's new? Maybe to adults. They had to rebuild it after a truck crashed through the deck into the Waimoana. Grandad Alan and his friend Tipene dived in and saved the driver's life.

Anyway, I walk to the rocks where people used to swim before the river changed course yet again, and where Grandad and Tipene found the carving. I sit there and read or think. Or I wander past the old orchard.

A scary thing happened to me one time in the orchard.

I was eleven. I'd finished a round of chemo, and was nearly ready to go back to school. Mum and I decided to go for a slow walk down to the orchard, so she could get a few pears.

We waited for Mr Ross from up the valley to drive over the bridge, then we crossed. We climbed the fence opposite where the roadman's cottage used to be (it fell down in an earthquake when Great-nana Florence was about my age), and started down the track towards the riverbed. Mum held my hand, in case I fell and grazed myself. I was fine on my own, but I've learned to let people do things that make them feel better about me. Hope that makes sense!

The orchard trees are all covered with lichen and moss now. They don't grow much fruit, but Mum likes to go there. Great-great-grandad Duncan was clearing the bush for the orchard when he almost lost his leg. Great-nana Florence and her friend Whina were there when the huge earthquake hit. It's a special place.

Under the trees, the world was green and quiet and clean-smelling. About forty metres away, the Waimoana glittered past. The riverbed boulders shimmered in the sun; a swallow flicked above them, doing wing-stands while it chased insects. Sometimes, living in our valley is just magic. Mum and I smiled at each other.

'I'll help you pick,' I told her.

'All right, love. Be careful.' I reckon people say 'Be careful' to me about fifty times a day.

'Quardle-aardle-oodle!' someone else went. I started to go 'Eh?', then realised it was the magpies telling one another that strange creatures with no wings were nearby.

Mum began reaching for the pears. I did the same, went 'Aw, yuk!' as I saw the caterpillar holes. 'Good for you,' Mum laughed. 'Full of protein.'

She stretched up towards a higher branch, and the silver bracelet around her wrist shone. Nana Beth passed it on to her a long while ago, and Mum gives it to me every time I'm going in for treatment. It's one of our family treasures, just like the little greenstone bat that her Maori friends Marika and Marama share between them.

We moved on towards another tree. A couple of magpies sat on a poplar branch a few metres away, watching us. 'Hi,' I went. 'Oodle-aardle,' they went. One of them took off; shot into the leaves somewhere ahead.

The pears were higher on the next tree. 'I'll drop them down to you,' Mum said, and began climbing. 'I can do—' I started. She interrupted. 'I know you can, but you won't.' I pushed my bottom lip out and pretended to sulk. My mother laughed. 'Careful. The wind might change, and then your face will be stuck like that.' Weird!

Thop! A pear landed on the grass. *Thup!* A second landed in my hands. *Dop!* A third landed on my head.

'Beware of Mad Mothers!' I yelled. Mum got the giggles, and had to hold onto the trunk.

Another half-dozen pears. We had a pretty good load; the bag was half-full by now. Mum clambered back down. 'One more tree,' she said.

The one ahead was thick and bushy. A clump of leaves and twigs was caught on a branch partway up.

Flap-Flap-Flap! The second magpie rose from the poplar, flashed around the tree my mother was heading for. 'Get lost!' I told it. I won't repeat what it told me.

Mum disappeared up into the branches. She's pretty fit for a . . . a mother. More pears began dropping into the grass. I stayed out of the road, just in case another one bounced off my skull. 'There's heaps up here,' Mum called down. 'We'll have stewed pears and pear salad and pear sandwiches and pear-burgers!'

'Yuk!' I went again, and started gathering up the ones she'd picked. I held them between finger and thumb in case there were any caterpillars. I wasn't scared. I just didn't want to hurt the caterpillars.

Flap-FLAP! One of the magpies thwacked past, just a metre away. 'Vanish!' I yelled, and chucked a wormy pear after it. I called up to my mother, where she was nearly hidden by the branches. 'We've got enough, eh?'

'There's a couple of good ones just further up,' she said. Branches shook as she began pulling herself up past the clump of twigs and leaves. I bent to put another pear in the bag. And then the magpies went crazy.

FLA-FLAP! SKAAARK-SKRAAAARK! They came crashing into the tree at my mother, both of them, wings thumping and smacking. Black beaks gaped; yellow eyes stared. Next second, they were storming and clawing around her head. I glimpsed her arms go up to protect her face; heard her yell.

Suddenly, I realised what the clump of twigs must be. 'A nest!' I shouted. 'That's their nest up there. Get down!'

I started towards the trunk. Up in the branches, Mum yelled and punched at the furious birds with one hand. Their wings struck at her face as they shrieked. One had its claws in her hair, stabbing at her neck with its big, dagger-shaped beak.

I seized a pear from the bag, and flung it up into the tree. 'Get off! Get away!' I hurled another. It ricocheted off a branch; the magpie on Mum's head squawked and let go. She came sliding and falling down the trunk, landed in the long grass on all fours. Her hair was a mess; her eyes stared. 'Get out — of here!' she panted.

Flap-FLAP! The maddened birds came at us again. A claw raked across my cheek; a feathered body whacked the top of my head. I screamed. 'Gerroff!'

Mum grabbed me with one hand, and the bag of pears with her other. Typical mother: even at a time like that, she was thinking about dessert. 'Keep your head down!' We stumbled towards the sunlight, out of the orchard. Wings tore past us once more.

Then we were clear of the trees. Behind us, two black and white maniacs dived back into the trees where their nest was. 'Beat them!' one squawked. 'Thrashed them!' went the second.

★

Mum and I stood among the round, grey stones of the riverbed, gasping and staring at each other. 'Maggie, your face is bleeding.' She put a finger on my cheek, and it came away wet and red. That claw flicking across my face. Lucky it hadn't got my eye.

'I'm fine.' And I *did* feel fine. I'd had an adventure. Now *I* had something to tell the kids at school about.

Mum still looked worried. 'Let's get you home and clean that up.' She was right: it's not just that you bleed easily if you've got leukaemia; since your immune system is all stuffed up, you can catch infections.

The bleeding was still going as we crossed the bridge. My elder brother, Cam, was helping Uncle John spray thistles in the home paddock. They stared when they saw us hurrying along, Mum's handkerchief pressed to my cheek. Cam dropped the spray-pack he held, and rushed towards us. 'You OK? What happened?'

'I'm fine,' I went again. 'Man, those magpies are killers!' He kept staring, and I realised how worried he was. Like I said, boys are pretty useless, and my brothers are especially useless. Sholto's only interested in computers and stuff; he should have shown Mum how to use the Web, but he couldn't be bothered. Cam's keen just on farming — and girls. But sometimes I understand that they do want to help me, and today was one of those times.

Uncle John was talking to Mum. 'Kate's got the car, Ailsa; it's the girls' jazz ballet lessons. But I can call Marama.'

My mother carefully lifted her handkerchief away from my cheek. 'It's stopping. I'll put antiseptic cream on it. We should be right.' She picked a couple of twigs from my hair; I wondered if I should mention that her own looked a bit like the magpies' nest. 'I was silly, love. And I was really silly to be wearing this.' She fingered the silver bracelet. 'They went for my hair clip when I was a kid. They must have been tossing up whether to grab or stab just now!'

So yeah, that was an adventure, all right. And I did tell the kids at school.

★

Just as well I wasn't wearing the bracelet, though. A few stabs on the hand or wrists from those evil beaks and I could have been in trouble. The hospital has blood transfusions ready for me if I ever cut myself badly, but I haven't used them yet, and I hope I never will. I heard Cam tell Mum once that if I ever needed blood, he wanted to help. Sholto went 'Me, too', even though he was too young to properly understand. I didn't say anything, but I reckon that was neat.

Mind you, my bros owe me a transfusion. One time a few years ago, when we were arguing over who could choose the TV programmes, I lost my temper and yelled 'You guys only want to watch stupid wrestling stuff like *Royal Rumble*. They've got even less brains than you two!' Cam gave me a shove; I thumped against the edge of the living-room door, and the whole top part of my right arm came up in this huge purple swelling: a haematoma, they call it.

Mum had to rush me into the hospital, so they could use ice to bring it down, and make sure it wasn't spreading. When we got home about four hours later, Cam's face was white and Sholto had been crying. 'I'm really sorry,' my big brother mumbled. 'I didn't mean to.' And Sholto said: 'You can choose the TV programmes all next week.'

I told them it was OK, and that night we watched *Royal Rumble*! It was quite funny, these enormous guys called The Big Boss Man and Hulk Hogan chucking one another out of the ring. I enjoyed it, though I didn't let on.

So, like I say, my brothers do care about me. It's just that they're boys, so they haven't evolved very much, and they can't help the way they are.

★

The evening after the mad magpies, Marama came over and said she and Marika wanted me to wear the little greenstone bat for a few days. 'It heals,' she told me. 'It protects. And from what I hear, you need protecting!'

The bat isn't the only greenstone being worn by Maori people in our valley now. Since Grandad Alan's friend Tipene, plus his sister Finola, helped start up a carving centre at Waimoana Marae, a lot of marvellous pendants and ear-rings and other things have been made. In the foyer at our primary school, there's this amazing carving of a ponga frond ready to uncurl that Tipene and others did. You see people with carved tiki or koru shapes around their necks. It's great.

One time, Marika and Marama took Mum and me to watch while a block of pounamu (greenstone) from the South Island was brought onto the marae. There were prayers and speeches, and this beautiful, glowing green boulder was placed on a woven cloak in the middle of the meeting house. It looked magic. So I believe that Marama and Marika's bat can heal and protect. I believe it can do anything.

★

There are other changes in our valley. Farming is

different now. People don't eat as much meat and cheese as they used to. Wool and leather aren't as important for clothes and blankets. So farms around Waimoana can't rely on just sheep and cattle.

Grandad Alan keeps goats, for their special milk. The Rosses tried farming alpacas, but Kylie Ross said they got tired of being spat on! So they changed to deer. Some farm cottages have been turned into bed-and-breakfast places. If I stay on in the valley (and if I live long enough: I have to keep facing that, but I'm going to make it!), I wonder what it'll be like then?

Hey, maybe I'll grow vegetables! How exciting is that? Marama is married to a guy called Tranh. He and his family are from Vietnam, and when they arrived they started a market garden. Now they grow bok choi and broccolini, and other stuff that Cam and Sholto won't eat.

Tranh is cool. He let me help in the garden; even said I could cut cauliflowers. 'Be careful,' he grinned. 'You cut off your finger, your mother cut off my head!' I think Mum was keen on him once, but Marama got there first. Their daughter Sheree is beautiful (and spoilt). Wish I had eyes and skin like her.

When I read Great-great-uncle Robert McDougall's book about Waimoana, I realised how many other things have changed. There's our 'new' bridge. There's families from other countries, like Tranh's. Dr Koen, the South African guy from the hospital, has a sister who's started a vineyard and café on the road to town. Some Fijian people live in what used to be a sharemilker's house between us and the marae; Mr Nadolo drives trucks for contractors.

It's the same over where Dad comes from. For ages, it was just Maori and Scottish people there. 'We all got along fine,' my father told me. 'Except for the bagpipes.' (There's stories about that in Great-great-uncle Robert's book.) Now they've got a Sri Lankan doctor, and Cambodian cleaners, and a Pakistani accountant, and a family from Sudan in Africa, who came because there's war in their country.

Other changes in our valley? The Waimoana Store closed down about five years ago. Shops in town are allowed to open on Sundays now, and most people drive in there, especially since the council straightened out the last tight corners on the road. Great-nana Florence reckons it's too easy to get everywhere now, but since I get car-sick after chemo, I don't mind.

The War Memorial Hall is still there. A Governor or someone opened it, would you believe? But it's only used for weddings or family reunions. Waimoana School has just one-and-two-quarter teachers now. (The two-quarters are Grandad Alan and Nana Beth; they take it in turns to help with the seniors. When I was there, I never knew which one of them might be in the classroom.) The roll has gone way down, because families are smaller, plus machines do most farm work now. And since it's so easy to drive into town, some parents send their kids to school there.

Great-great-uncle Robert McDougall's book describes how the school used to be much bigger; how it was one of the first to bring in Maori people to teach their language and games and history. Now that's all coming back; little Waimoana led the way!

Like I say, it'd be brilliant to write a book, the way Uncle Robert and Finola did. Or to be a doctor. Whatever I do, I want to help people. Such a lot of them have helped me.

There's one place that always changes, yet it stays the same. I'm talking about the cemetery. I spend a lot of time up there. If that sounds sick (me sick? Haha: *sick* joke), then Mum says she used to wander around there when she was trying to sort things out after Dad and she split. She and Grandad Alan, and Great-nana Florence until she died, keep it tidy. Uncle John sprays the weeds; even Cam and Sholto help sometimes, when they're not being stupid boys.

Just about everyone who's died in our valley is in our cemetery, though more Maori people are buried in the urupa up the hill near their marae. Quite a few people get cremated now, but they usually still have a plaque or something. I like reading them; I know some off by heart.

It's peaceful being up there. You can still hear tractors and haybalers working in the paddocks, or rumbling over our 'new' bridge. There's even a few hoon cars come tearing through. That's another change in the valley; I'll talk about it later.

Magpies and other birds tell the world they're in charge. Some days, the wind booms in the macrocarpas nearby, and if it's rained for a while, you can hear the river rumbling along in its bed. I think of Grandad Alan and Tipene when that happens. But the cemetery always seems quiet.

Walking around and reading the graves makes me feel better, somehow. There's people here who drowned or died in a big 'flu epidemic years back, or were killed in farm accidents. There's a headstone for a guy who died in World War One. My Great-great-uncle Angus, who was killed trying to help people in the Tangiwai train crash, is here. I'm lucky.

And I feel like I'm surrounded by friends. Yeah, that's *really* sick, but when I see the names of all our family, reaching back over a hundred years — Duncan . . . Lily . . . Jess . . . John . . . Niall . . . Aggie, who I'm named after . . . Big Angus (those last names are hard to read now), and when I read the names of their friends: Whina . . . Rawiri . . . Ahorangi . . . Hahona, I know that every one of them would be on my side, would want to help me if they could.

I feel better in other ways, too. Being in the cemetery makes me realise that dying is just ordinary. It happens to everyone, sooner or later. (*Remember! You read it here first! Nobody else ever thought of this before!*) I don't feel like I'm on the outside, the way I sometimes do if my chemo is going badly, or if I get scared. You're born; you do the best you can; then sooner or later, you die. I'm going to make sure it's later for me, remember? But our cemetery helps me face up to things.

Sometimes when I think about what happened to people in our family — sailing all the way from Scotland, going blind, accidents, wars, earthquakes, protest marches — I don't seem to have done anything in my life. Like I said, hardly any adventures. Except . . . you can have adventures in your mind as well. I see and hear. I think and I imagine. Heaps happens to me!

Just being in my family is an adventure. Remember how I said I'd love to play rugby for the Black Ferns? Well, even though she marched against the Springbok Tour back before I was born, my mum is a real rugby fan, too. Just about every All Blacks game, she's in front of the TV, cheering and booing. I'm usually there, too — watching her as much as the game!

Uncle John says that when New Zealand won the very first Rugby World Cup in 1987, Mum and Auntie Kate charged around the lawn afterwards, yelling and dancing. Wish I could have seen that. They haven't done much dancing since then; the ABs have been knocked out of every World Cup. Wonder if we'll ever win again?

★

There's other stuff I want to do. When Dad came to visit me and Mum a couple of months back, he told us how some of his aunts and uncles have been back to Scotland to look up their relatives. His family came out to New Zealand for the same reasons as Mum's: to make better lives. Some of them stayed behind. Some who set out died from disease on the voyage, or their ship caught fire or sank in a storm. Now those families are meeting up again. That's amazing. I'm going to do something like that when I'm well.

I was thinking about this the other day, while I sat on the rocks near where Grandad Alan and Tipene found the little carved panel. (And where they almost drowned. I can imagine my silly brothers doing something like that.)

The rocks are another of my favourite places. I like swimming there, although I have to be careful not to scrape myself. The river made a new bed after the huge flood that swept the carving down. It's shifted again lots of times since then. The weather is different, some scientists say. They're talking about — what is it? — climate change, which I don't really understand.

So there's heaps of new things going on in our quiet little place. They're not all good. I've heard stories how some gangs have been planting marijuana away up in the hills. Maybe that's why those hoon cars are around? A couple of times, I've seen helicopters flying slowly up the valley; they look as if they're searching. Mum shook her head one time when we were out in the garden, and a chopper smacked its way overhead. 'Dopes growing dope!' she muttered.

Just before Guy Fawkes Night last year, Mum and I were asleep when I half-heard this *WHOOMPFF!* from somewhere. I lay and listened. A car accident? Another earthquake? A bunch of cows deep-breathing?

I heard it again. *WHOOMPFF!* It was coming from down by the river.

Mum's light blinked on. Cam and Sholto didn't wake up, of course. 'Mum?' I called out. 'Did you hear that?'

She came into my room. I could see her pulling on her dressing-gown.

'I'll take a look, love. Can't imagine what it was.'

I was already sliding out of bed. 'Can I come, too?'

Mum hesitated. 'All right. But be careful, Maggie. I don't want you falling over in the dark and bruising yourself.'

We stood on the back path. It was a clear, still night. The Southern Cross hung low and bright over the cemetery. Dad taught me all about the constellations, and I could see the curve of Scorpius the Scorpion setting on one side of the sky, while Orion the Hunter climbed up over the horizon. Our trees were dark shadows. A morepork called from somewhere; otherwise there wasn't a sound. The world was silent and magic.

Mum walked to the back gate and stood looking towards the river. I joined her, moving carefully like she said, and felt her relax when I arrived. No more noises: what had they been?

After a couple of minutes, I shivered. Straightaway, Mum whipped me inside, made sure I was all right, and sent me back to bed. I felt disappointed; it had been so cool, standing outside with her under those glittering stars. Hey, I'd wait until she was asleep, then sneak out for another look. I closed my eyes to rest them for a minute while she dozed off. I opened my eyes a couple of minutes later, and the sun was glowing into my room.

We were all having breakfast when Uncle John knocked on the door. 'Can I borrow the boys for a while, Ailsa? There's a bit of a mess down on the riverbed.'

We stared. My uncle shook his head. 'Some stupid sod's been chucking dynamite in the water. Too bloody lazy to go fishing properly. There's dead whitebait and eels all over the place.'

He was right. We trooped across the paddock and over the stile to the bridge. Auntie Kate was there. Marama and pretty, spoilt Sheree arrived. My mother's friend sounded angry. 'That's so disgusting! Wish I could catch the idiots who did it!'

The shallow water at the river's edge was dotted with the bodies of fish, killed by the dynamite. Now I knew what those *WHOOMPFF!* sounds had been in the night. I wished I could catch the morons who'd done it, too. I'd . . . I'd like to try some of their own dynamite out on them.

Uncle John, Cam and Sholto spent an hour down at the riverbed, gathering up the dead eels and whitebait. Sheree stood on the bridge and watched the boys. Mum wouldn't let me help. If anything dead gets into my skin, it could start an infection.

'Some of them had their guts blown out,' Cam told Mum and me later. 'But most of them — you'd never know they were dead at first look.' His face was tight, and for the first time I could see that my silly big brother just might grow up into a strong, tough man.

'Nothing like this has ever happened before,' sighed Grandad Alan, when I went over to his and Nana Beth's cottage to tell them. He shook his head, just like my uncle had done. 'There's people around now who don't care about anyone or anything. We can't let them spoil this place; it's too precious.'

Uncle John dug most of the dead fish into his vegetable garden; got Sholto and Cam to dig the rest into ours. 'At least it'll make good fertiliser.' I watched as the bodies were tipped into trenches in the soil. The eels still glistened black and green in the morning sun. The whitebait's eyes stared; their mouths were open. They looked so tiny, and so perfect. I tried to imagine someone doing a thing like that, just because they couldn't be bothered using a fishing line or a net. Whoever had done this deserved — Uncle John expression coming — a boot up the backside.

Those were some of the things I thought about this morning as I sat on the warm rocks, gazing up the river. The flax bushes and reeds of the swamp glowed in the early sun. A single hawk drifted above them. Marama and Marika say it keeps watch. Their Nana Whina reckons that as long as a hawk — a kahu — is guarding the swamp, it'll be safe.

There's going to be some digging at the swamp by a university group. They'll see if there's any signs of things hidden there. There was another excavation that Great-grandad Matiu helped with, years and years ago, but they didn't find anything.

Now a lot of people from the marae are exploring their own past, wanting to make sure their stories are told properly. Great-uncle Tipene's wife, my Great-auntie Pania, is one. There were meetings on the marae, lots of talk. Grandad Alan and Nana Beth went along; Grandad took the wooden stick that Tipene had carved for him. Nana says he held it while he spoke, and his friend was so pleased. Grandad said the swamp was one of the taonga — the treasures — of the land, and he would support whatever the marae decided. So yeah, there's going to be another excavation, starting next month.

I had this really strange thought while I was sitting gazing at the swamp. I was pretty tired, like I've been for the past couple of weeks, and a bit dreamy, I suppose.

Anyway, I started wondering: whose valley is this? Is it *my* valley? Somebody like Great-great-aunt Whina: was it *her* valley? Is it Tipene and Pania's? Or Aggie's, after whom I'm named?

I'd wondered about something like it before, when I was in the cemetery, reading all those names from years and years back. Did those people ever stand by the river, and look around like me, and think 'This is my place. I belong to it; it belongs to me'? I guess they must have — though some of them were guys, so they probably didn't do much thinking.

If they did, they were right. They and Waimoana belonged to each other while they were alive. Then the valley belonged to those who came after them, and the ones who came after that. It belongs to everybody, and to nobody.

Pretty amazing, eh? The idea, I mean, not my thinking. It's the sort of thing I'd like to write about, when I'm a bit older.

My bum was getting sore from all the sitting and thinking. I've got a skinny bum; girls at high school say they wish they were as slim as me. Then they remember the leukaemia; they go red and don't know what to say. I just laugh.

I stood up, and began heading towards the bridge and home. Like I said, I felt tired. It happens. Dr Koen's been talking to Mum about this new treatment, where they take some of your DNA and use it to rebuild healthy cells in your body. That's another thing they can do for me if they need to.

I stopped halfway along the bridge and looked around, trying to take everything in like I was seeing it for the first time. The Waimoana glittered among the riverbed stones. A couple of magpies, probably rellies of those thugs who beat Mum and me up, did a show-off forward-roll in mid-air, then flashed back to their tree. The hawk still hung high above the swamp.

I heard Mum telling Uncle John one time how she'd decided on the way home from a protest march that living here was a treasure. She saw me listening, and shut up. Why? Because in a few years, I might *not* be living — here or anywhere else. Meanwhile, my uncle went 'Aw, yeah. Good one, Ailsa.' Typical male!

What do I think? I guess Mum's right. I guess a lot of people have thought the same. I reckon every day is like discovering something new and special. You never know what you'll find. You never know when you'll meet someone or something that changes your life.

Did I just write that? How embarrassing. How puke-making. But it's true. Every day is my treasure. I'm gonna make the most of them. And I'm gonna live years and years and *years* of them. Betya!

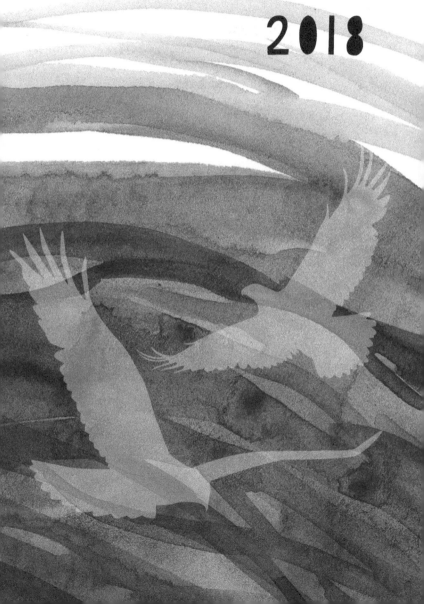

CALLUM

2018

They're going to make up their minds this morning. I just know they are.

They've been talking about it for months now: Dad and Mum, Nana Ailsa and Great-uncle John, Uncle Sholto when he can drive over from his farm-adviser job, Grandad Robbie has Skyped a few times (he works in the Pacific Islands, on health and environment things), and he's told Dad that whatever people decide, he'll support them 100 per cent.

We might be leaving the farm — selling it (if Dad and Uncle Sholto can get a buyer) and moving into town. It's hard to believe. Melody — I'll tell you more about Melody later — and her Nana Marama came over a week back. Mum was all worked up about our maybe leaving, and she started crying while she talked to Marama. And while Melody and I kept looking at each other and pretending not to look.

'Cam's family have lived here for 130 years,' Mum sobbed. 'Mine, too.' My mother was a Sheffield; one of her great-great-uncles or something used to own a big place further up the valley. 'Your family has helped us for all that time. I can't bear to think of moving away. Leaving all the old ones up there in the cemetery — it feels like we're betraying them.'

Marama put her arms around Mum, went 'I know, Tessa. I know. But it's not decided yet, is it?' Mum sniffed, and shook her head, and tried to smile, while Melody and I sneaked another look at each other.

★

I first heard them talking about leaving just before the time capsule was buried.

Yeah, we've got a time capsule. It's a metal box, actually, inside another metal box, buried beside the main entrance to Waimoana School, with a sign to show where it is. It's to mark 100 years since the end of World War One. The idea is that people in another 100 years will dig it up, and look at it, and probably go 'Man, they were *so* old-fashioned!'

They were going to bury the capsule at one end of the bridge, since that had a Historic Places plaque put on it a few years back. Then they talked about putting it beside the War Memorial Hall, though that's hardly used these days. But Great-grandad Alan and Great-nana Beth, and their friends Tipene and Pania from the marae reckoned the capsule is about the past *and* the future, and so is the school, so that was the best place.

Plus Waimoana School is really buzzing again. People from town send their kids out to it, and it's pretty famous because of the way it teaches Maori language and history and stuff. We've got our own Kohanga Reo for little kids. Nana and Grandad say Maori people in the valley have always helped with the school, right back to when it started.

And here's something else amazing. One of my teachers when I went there was Ms Graham. She's the principal now. But the thing is, she's the great-great-niece of Mr McDougall (I'll tell you more about him later, too), and *he* was the grand-nephew of another Mr McDougall, who was the school's very first teacher. Is that cool, or is that weird and cool?

Back to the time capsule. Yeah, back to the future! What's in it? Heaps of stuff; they just about needed another box. There's a copy of the book that Mr McDougall (who's Ms Graham's great-and-so-on uncle) wrote about our valley. There's what Aunt Maggie wrote before she died. There's some newspapers from this year. There's photos and DVDs showing the bridge when a huge earthquake almost wrecked it; the river in flood; old farms and roads; hundreds of people going right back to when cameras were invented, just about. There's a carving from the swamp. Not the famous one that Great-grandad Alan and Tipene found; that's still kept on the marae.

★

A couple of other things nearly ended up in the capsule. One was the bracelet from Scotland, with the silver thistle and patterns on it, the one that women and girls in our family have always worn. Nana Ailsa talked about burying it after Auntie Maggie was killed.

Yeah, killed. She had leukaemia when she was a kid, but she was all recovered by the time I was born. She started writing stories and magazine articles about it, because she'd always wanted to be an author. Quite a few got published.

Then one morning, when I must have been about four or five, she was coming back across the road from the cemetery. She spent a lot of time there, Dad says; reckoned it made her feel peaceful and gave her things to write about. This half-stoned guy in a hoon car came tearing around the corner towards the bridge, on the wrong side of the road, and hit her.

She usually wore the bracelet when she went to the cemetery, but that morning she hadn't. Mum says Nana Ailsa couldn't look at the bracelet for a long time; wanted to get rid of it. 'It's so unfair!' she kept going. 'After all Maggie went through. It's so wrong!' So she wanted to put the bracelet in the time capsule. But Marama and her twin sister Marika, and their mother Pania, said that if that happened, then the little greenstone bat their family always wore was going in with it. 'Pekapeka and thistle: they have bound us together.' Nana Ailsa didn't say much, but she kept the bracelet.

★

The guy whose car killed my aunt went to jail for five years. But he met with Nana and Mum and Dad and the rest of our family. He said it was his fault, and he knew he couldn't ever bring their sister and daughter back, but he promised to spend the rest of his life trying to make up for it. So he should. But OK, he did the right thing.

Dad didn't want to listen to him at first, until Nana Ailsa went: 'Remember Sheree, Cam.' Sheree is Marama's daughter; Melody's mother. She lives somewhere in town; she's been on drugs ever since she was a teenager. Dad went out with her a few times before he met Mum, and he tried dope, too. He stopped; Sheree didn't, and they split up. Even after Melody was born, Sheree kept using, until Marama took her daughter away. She's a mess.

You'd never guess my father used to be young and pretty wild. He's so . . . respectable. He did finally come to the meeting with the driver, the restorative justice session. Now the guy's out of prison, and he works for anti-drug projects. Pity a few others I've seen around the valley aren't like him.

★

Anyway, like I was saying about a thousand pages back, we could be leaving the farm. By the time I got back home today, they'd have made up their minds.

All the adults were meeting at our place. I don't think there'd been so many there since we watched the All Blacks win the World Cup (third time!). Mum and Dad, of course; Nana Ailsa; Great-uncle John and Great-aunt Kate; Uncle Sholto. Great-nana Beth lives in a flat in town now, but she was coming out. Grandad Robbie had Skyped, like I said.

My annoying little sister Meg had gone over to the marae for the day to be with her friend Mita, and I knew the olds didn't want me there, in case there were any major arguments. So I said I was going down to the riverbed. Dad reckons everyone in our family goes down there when they need time out.

I crossed the home paddock towards the stile that takes you onto the road and bridge. Aunt Maggie was heading back this way when she was killed. Nana Ailsa walked the long way to the cemetery for ages; she couldn't bear to be on that stretch of road.

I whacked the tops off a few thistles as I went. We haven't had enough money to spray them this year, so I smash any I see. I found this stick a couple of weeks ago, down by the rocks where people swim — if the river hasn't shifted. It makes a cool thistle-slayer.

That reminded me. (A lot of things seemed to be reminding me today.) One other thing almost went in the time capsule — it was the walking stick that our family's had forever. It used to be part of an axe that almost cut my three-times-Great-grandad Duncan's leg off, when he was clearing bush for the orchard. He nearly died. A long time later, Melody's great-grandad carved it into this brilliant walking stick. Great-grandad Alan used it when he was old. When he died, not long before the capsule was buried, people talked about leaving the stick to be found in a hundred years. But — well, it was way too long for the capsule!

So our family gave it to the marae to keep. We all took it across. Melody and her Nana Marama and Marika and others welcomed us and sang. Oh man, Melody looked brilliant. Her grandad came from Vietnam as a refugee, and she's got these amazing dark eyes and cheekbones.

Then Nana Ailsa said: 'Our ancestor's axe cut down your trees. In return, one of *your* ancestors turned this handle into a treasure. We hope it helps you shape the new life on your marae.' I thought that was pretty brilliant, too.

There were more speeches, and Pania made some joke about how pleased she was not to hear any bagpipes this time; don't ask me why. Then we all had lunch, and I tried to think of something cool to say to Melody.

★

So today, I headed for the bridge. Nobody was up at the cemetery. Nana and Mum have been working up there a lot, these past few weeks, tidying up the graves. Meg helped sometimes, which was pretty good — for her.

When I was in Year 6, our class did a history project on the cemetery. The very first people from our family, who came out from Scotland in the 1880s, are there, though it's hard to read their names now. One of them, called Aggie (Aunt Maggie was named after her) went blind on the ship bringing them out. How could you live like that? The same way Aunt Maggie lived with her cancer, I guess. I wonder how those first people felt, coming halfway across the world to our valley? Wonder how *I'll* feel if we're the last ones to live here?

We're thinking of moving because it's got harder and harder to make a living from farming. People here have tried everything: alpacas, goats, deer. A few do OK: the market gardens that Melody's Vietnamese grandparents started mean some jobs. But most places struggle. Mum and Dad tried turning Great-nana Beth's farm cottage into a bed-and-breakfast, but not many people came. We're too close to town, I suppose. Dad drives the school bus to earn a few extra bucks. Mum works part-time for a rural women's welfare thing.

The river slid by beneath me, in its shingle bed. A truck crashed through our bridge into the water one time, nearly fifty years back. Great-grandad Alan and his friend Tipene got the driver out. They were real heroes for a while. Wish I could do something like that.

I had to hurry over the last part of the bridge. This car came onto the deck behind me — fast. A black one with tinted windows. It didn't slow down when it saw me, so I ran the last few metres and swung myself up onto the rails at the side. I could just make out two guys inside as the car hooned past. I think they were laughing; I didn't recognise them.

There's some tricky people around Waimoana now. The ones on the new lifestyle blocks are friendly enough, even if they're a bit snobby. But everyone knows there's dope being grown in the bush away up at the head of the valley. Farmers or hunters find it sometimes. The cops send out choppers to search for it. I stared after the black car as it barrelled on around the corner. I thought about giving it the fingers, but decided not to. If we do leave the farm, I'd sooner leave it alive.

One weekend, my mate Nathan came out from town with this drone that he and his father had put together. We took it down by the river, and got it flying. 'We should look for pot plantations,' Nathan said.

'Yeah, and what would you do if you found one?'

Nathan shrugged. 'Keep my mouth shut, probably.'

I'd tell Dad. We've talked about it. He said if anyone offers me dope, I can always tell them I've got this medical condition, and I'll get really sick if I smoke it. Nobody's given me any, luckily.

The drone was cool. We went over to the rocks, where you get a good view up the river, to see how far we could send it. It went buzzing away towards the swamp.

A hawk hovered in the sky above the flax and reeds. There's always a hawk there: never more than one. It came swooping down towards the drone, and Nathan yelled 'Aw, no! It'll smash it!' But the big bird just circled once, then glided back over the swamp. We turned the drone away.

Then on Monday, I just happened to sit down across the aisle of the school bus from Melody, and she went 'Hi, Callum. Someone was flying one of those drone things up the river on Saturday.'

I opened my mouth to say that I was the expert pilot, and she should come and watch us. But she was still talking. 'Nana says some of the elders at the marae were upset. The swamp is special. They don't like the idea of anyone invading it.'

She didn't say any more; just gave me the smile that makes my stomach flip. I decided then and there I'd never fly any drones again. 'Girls can do anything,' Nana Ailsa keeps saying, and I reckon Melody can . . . well, she can make *me* do anything!

★

I've known her all our lives. Her mother, Sheree, used to park her with her Nana Marama and go off with boyfriends. Our families go to heaps of things together — weddings, anniversaries, that sort of stuff. She's got a little brother called Kahu, which means 'hawk', and Meg tries to boss him around. Kahu wants to be a carver, too. Maybe when I'm a hundred, I'll have made my mind up what I want to do. Actually, I've got a couple of ideas.

I began to drop down on the other side of the railings, then stopped as I saw the rural post van come around the corner where the black car had vanished. Melody's Nana Marama drives it; that's her way of earning a bit extra. She slowed and wound down her window. 'Hello, Callum. Nice day, eh? I'm just going to deliver six parcels and pick up one grand-daughter.' What time are you coming back? I almost asked, but she'd gone.

The riverbed shone in the morning sun. Sometimes it's so fresh and clean, with the stones and water, and trees on the banks, that I want to stand there and remember everything about it. I never say anything like that to my mates, of course.

But one thing I'd like to do is write about this place. I like reading; I'm pretty good at English. Mum reckons I've got some of Aunt Maggie's genes. I like Earth and Space Studies, too. Dad says the weather is different these days: more storms, longer droughts. That makes farming harder, too. I could write something about climate change and how it's affecting our valley.

The Waimoana gurgled along under the bank. On days like this, it was hard to believe the floods that almost killed people, the times when just slipping as you waded across could mean death. Most rivers are like that, I guess. Another one killed Nana Ailsa's Great-uncle Angus when the train he was on crashed into it. And I saw a kid from high school nearly die in ours.

It was just over a year ago. I was heading down for a swim, and I was in a bad mood because I had to look after Meg. My bad mood got badder when I saw a flash car parked just past the far end of the bridge, and heard voices yelling down on the riverbed. Townies, or maybe one of the lifestyle blocks (though most of them have their own pools). What made them think they could just drive out and use our river?

My badder mood got gooder when Meg and I were crossing the stones, and I saw Melody sitting by the water's edge. Kahu was with her; she must have been given baby-sitting duty, too. She wore gold-coloured togs; she looked amazing.

Meg rushed over, and started ordering Kahu around,

as usual. He grinned and took no notice, as usual. I couldn't think of anything cool to say to Melody, as usual. She gave me that smile, nodded at the yelling from just downstream, and said 'Noisy, eh?'

There were two guys and two girls: must have come in that flash car. They were a few years older than us, Year 12 or 13. Right then, one of the guys — he was standing high up on the far bank above the deep part — called 'Kamikaze!' and did this enormous, look-at-me dive into the river. His mate yelled 'Go, Luke!' The girls, who sat in the shallow water making sure their hair didn't get wet, cheered and squealed.

Luke: I recognised the guy. He was from our high school. Year 13, one of the super-cool studs who've always got girls hanging around them. I recognised one of the girls, too: the loudest squealer.

The second guy started scrambling up towards where Luke had dived. 'They need to be careful,' Melody murmured. 'The bank slopes out under the water.'

She was right. You couldn't see it because of the current, but there was a bulge that swelled out for nearly a metre, just below the surface. You've got to make sure you land well out from the bank.

The second guy worked his way up a bit higher than Luke had, did a couple of ape-man yells, then dived, too. The girls squealed louder. I opened my mouth, closed it again as he came up, spluttering and laughing.

Luke pulled himself out onto the far bank. He was

tall and muscly, just like I want to be. 'Call that high?' he shouted to his mate, and began scrambling up the slope again.

'He shouldn't—' Melody started to stand, but I was already wading into the river. 'I'll tell him.' I started swimming across towards the far bank, right under where Luke was getting ready to dive.

He glared down at me. 'Move, kid.' *Kid?* Who did he think—

'Watch out,' I called. 'The bank sticks out here. It's pretty dangerous.'

The girls had started shrieking and squealing again. The other guy was yelling, too. Luke kept glaring. 'You've got three seconds, son.'

I hauled myself along in the water until I was out of his way. He came off the high bank in a perfect dive, while the squeals rose even louder, and knifed into the river. I saw the shape of him jolt sideways as he thumped into the underwater bulge.

I was already swimming towards him as he came to the surface. From where the others were, it probably looked like an ordinary dive, but I could see his eyes staring, his mouth gaping open. He grunted for breath, struggled to stay afloat. As I reached him, he started to go under again.

I grabbed his elbow, shoved him towards the bank. He grabbed a tree root and clung to it, sucked in air, shuddering and jerking. 'You OK?' I went. The girls had gone silent; the other guy called out something. 'You OK?' I asked again.

He — Luke — pulled himself away from me. 'Stuff — off!' He splashed towards the shallows, awkwardly and slowly. The guy was tough; he must have given himself a real whack against the bank, but he was trying not to show it.

He reached the far shore; stood hunched over, looking shaky. One of the girls asked something; he jerked his head at her. After a few seconds, he went 'C'mon, Jordy, let's move. This place sucks.' The second guy stared, then swam across to join him. Luke didn't look at me. Melody sat silently. Meg was still trying to boss Kahu around.

The four of them left soon after. I heard a voice going 'What a dump . . . losers' as they passed behind us. I didn't care. As I'd sat down, Melody had gone 'You all right, Callum?' and touched my hand. Oh man, I could have dived back in and rescued another *ten* idiots!

I thought about all that while I wandered along the riverbed. Back at our house, Dad and Mum and the others would be making up their minds. Maybe they had already. Maybe in a few months I'd be living somewhere in town?

That could be OK. I'd still see Melody at school. My parents would come out a lot to visit friends and the marae, and I'd make sure I came with them. Anyway, it was less than an hour on my bike — if there wasn't a head wind.

Yet in some ways, I've got most of the things I want right here in Waimoana. Plus I can text my mates to see about meeting up, although reception is a bit shaky sometimes. Not just cellphone reception: the satellite feed for our TV went on the blink just before the last Rugby World Cup final. Imagine if we hadn't been able to watch? Imagine if we're still here, and it happens during the *next* World Cup final! I want to see us win three times in a row.

Melody and Kahu and their nana all came over to watch the last game. She's a rugby fan. Aunt Maggie used to have a poster of the first-ever Black Ferns, the New Zealand women's rugby team, and after she was killed, Dad gave the poster to Melody.

Yeah, I know. Melody, Melody, Melody . . . But I can't talk to my mates about her; guys don't do that sort of stuff. So I'm talking to the paper. And to you.

She and some of the other girls on the bus sometimes sing in Maori on the way to school. Sing and giggle and whisper to one another, like girls do. It sounds quite cool — the singing part, that is.

I can speak a bit of Maori. Like I said, we all got taught some at primary school. I should try to learn more; maybe I could ask for some lessons from . . . Mustn't use that word.

You hear quite a few languages in town and even around Waimoana now. Vietnamese, of course; Chinese; people from countries like Serbia. Some Muslim refugee families have come; there's three girls at high school who wear head scarves with their uniforms. They look quite cute. Some kids called them Towel-Heads and A-rabs and crap like that, until the teachers jumped on them. There's always idiots around. I've heard Marama and Pania talk about the sneers that Maori people still get sometimes. Sometimes you hear stuff that makes you wonder if it'll *ever* stop.

I passed the terrace where our orchard used to be. A lawyer from town bought the land about five years back. Nana Ailsa and Great-uncle John agreed we really needed the money; milk prices were way down. But everyone hated selling it, Dad and Uncle Sholto especially. Now there's a concrete-and-glass house with a pool, and even a small vineyard where the grapes won't grow properly, ha ha.

When the contractors started dropping the old fruit trees, Dad and I went down to watch. Mum wouldn't come; Nana Ailsa stayed inside her cottage. I quite liked the bulldozers ripping at the ground, the branches thrashing, the way the roots seemed to try to hold onto the soil, then tear out as the whole tree crashed down. The air was full of dust and leaves. Magpies screeched and skidded all over the place. The contractor guys wore hard hats; from the look of the magpies, they might need them.

After about twenty minutes, Dad said 'Come on, Callum, son. That's enough.' I was going to ask if I could stay, but when I heard how his voice sounded and looked at his face, I kept my mouth shut.

★

The morning after the trees were all down, and the bulldozer had shoved them into a huge pile waiting to be burned, I went down by myself to search around. Magpies like shiny stuff; one of them went for the silver bracelet that Nana Ailsa was wearing while she picked fruit years back, and someone found a piece of paua nearby that might have come from a carving or something.

I picked my way around the broken branches and drifts of leaves. It was still hard to believe we'd never get any more plums or apples or pears from there again. OK, there'd been almost none for years; the trees were so old. But Nana Ailsa and Great-nana Beth said the orchard used to be a real treasure.

People have called all sorts of things around here 'treasure'. The swamp of course, and what they found there. Those ones who came here 130 years ago — what treasure did they imagine we'd find? Mr McDougall's book, the one in the time capsule, says it was the new land. Aunt Maggie wrote how just being alive was the most precious thing you could find. I've even heard Mum call my sister Meg 'Treasure'. (She's more like something from the $2 Shop, if you ask me.) But I realised a long time ago that there's nothing special to find around here.

Except . . . that morning after the orchard came down, I did find something. A pair of magpies were perched on the pile of smashed trunks and branches, squawking and flying up and watching me come. I didn't have a stick then like the one I carry now, but there were plenty I could grab if I needed to.

The birds squawked louder as I got near where one tree had been rooted out. They curved in a circle around me, screeching to each other. I stopped and stared down.

A bowl lay on the ground in front of me. A scruffy bowl made of twigs and grass. A nest. Four speckled blue eggs lay inside it.

I squatted down to look closer. The magpies shrieked, skimmed so low over my head, I felt their wings whack past. I glimpsed yellow eyes staring.

I picked the nest up, carefully. The two birds squawked and skidded by. I carried the little bowl and its eggs over to a big puriri tree the contractors must have been told to leave. Three metres up, two branches forked, with a hollow between them. I pulled myself up with my free hand. As gently as I could, I placed the nest in the fork, and wiggled it so it was held fast.

I slid back to the ground. Where were the magpies? Up above me in the puriri branches, perched silently, those yellow eyes watching me, dagger beaks half-open.

'There you are, boids,' I said. 'Say "thank you".' As I walked away, I heard a fluttering behind me. The magpies were checking the nest.

One of them called. It was a different call, like music. We'd read a poem at school, where magpies went 'Quardle oodle, ardle wardle doodle', and that was exactly the sound this one made. It was almost like they *were* saying 'thanks' to me, though I know that's stupid. But I felt sort of special.

I remembered all that today, as I looked at my watch. Back in our farmhouse, they must have made their minds up by now. What did I want? Town and exciting stuff? The valley and a certain person I could see in town, anyway? I was starting to make my mind up, too.

I reached the riverbed, and sent a couple of stones skimming across the water. I guess the nearest our valley ever got to real treasure was when Great-grandad Alan and Tipene found that carving. It's been kept on the marae ever since, and it's amazing: all scrolls and patterns and staring eyes. Every time I see it, I feel like the eyes know about me, somehow.

A university group came and dug in the swamp years ago. The marae had given them permission to search for anything that early Maori people might have hidden there after they came to Waimoana. They discovered a few more carvings: there's a big one, probably from over the doorway of a meeting house. Near the edge of the swamp were a few little wooden things that could have been spinning tops. Funny to think of kids playing there while their parents maybe did something mysterious and important.

Some of the stuff the university found stayed on the marae. Some went to the museum in town. The marae gave the big doorway carving to Te Papa. Then they said they didn't want any more excavation. The swamp was a treasure itself, and they didn't want it disturbed again. I reckon that's cool. But like I say, it means there's nothing new to be found here.

★

It was time to head back. Time to learn where and how I'd be living the next part of my life.

I stood still for a few seconds. I gazed around me, at the river, stones, the poplars downstream, the bridge, the old swimming place by the rocks. I tilted back my head, to let the sun shine on my face. I know it's just imagination, but the sun in our valley feels brighter and cleaner somehow than it does in town.

A shadow slid past overhead. A hawk, gliding towards the swamp. Must be its turn to stand guard there.

Be brilliant to fly: that was my incredibly intellectual thought as I headed towards the path up to the bridge. OK, I have flown a couple of times. Not with my wings: in a plane, up to Auckland to see some of Mum and Dad's rellies. We went to see where my too-many-greats-to-list-grandfather Duncan's sister Jess lived. She did all sorts of things to help improve women's wages and conditions. The government gave her a medal: an MBE, whatever that means. The new building where her house once stood is named after her.

Great-grandad Alan and Tipene had asked if we could visit the place where Finola used to be. She was Tipene's sister, and like Jess, though much younger. She wrote about Maori women's lives.

We couldn't find the place. Mum said it's too often

246

like that: Maori people aren't honoured the same way. 'It's still not an equal country, Callum. Remember that.' Yes, Mum.

I enjoyed the flights. One time, we came in over the Waimoana Valley. I saw everything: our farmhouse; the cottages and the cemetery; the bridge and the river glittering. Weird to think my whole life so far had fitted into that little space. My parents were gazing down, too — and holding hands. How puke-making.

That was the first flight home. The second time I saw . . . clouds.

There's a bunch of other families who came out from Scotland soon after ours. They live a couple of hundred ks away: we see them now and then. Some of them have flown to Scotland for a visit. I'd like to travel that far. Maybe when I make my mind up what I want to do; when I'm . . . 200?

Nana Ailsa has Skyped Scottish people who might be rellies of ours. One of them sent her a picture of this bird called an osprey. It looks so much like the hawk you see over our swamp.

The same woman asked Nana if she'd like to get her DNA tested, so they can work out how closely they're related: 'find out who you really are'.

Nana said she already knew who she was. She's a New Zealander. She's proud to be one, and proud to have Maori blood in her veins from her Grandad Matiu. I'm a New Zealander, too. And I'm proud to have my little bit of Maori blood.

It takes over twenty-four hours' flying time to reach Scotland from here, I heard a woman from one of those other families saying at Great-grandad Alan's funeral. It took nearly 130 *days* for the very first of our family to sail to New Zealand, Nana Ailsa told me and Meg one time.

Wish I could have met some of them. Aggie the blind one, and her friend Hahona. Duncan with the almost-cut-off leg and his friend Rawiri. Florence and Whina, who lived through the huge earthquake.

Some of them went away, like I might be doing. Niall (feels cheeky to call them just by their first names), who fought in the South African War, and whose horse found its way home from Wellington. Jess and her MBE.

Wonder if I'll ever do anything important enough to get an award? Not throttling Meg deserves an award, sometimes. Nah, I suppose she's all right — for a little sister.

I stopped again at the track up to the bridge, and looked around once more. This morning felt like I was seeing things for the last time. That's rubbish, 'cos even if Mum and Dad do decide to leave, we'll be here until they sell. But I felt like I almost knew already what they'd decided. And like we were all getting ready to go away.

A truck whirred across the deck above. Great-grandad Alan told me when I was small how the old wooden bridge used to clatter and bang when anything drove over it. 'Even a flea on a trike woke me up at night.' I was so young, I believed him.

He was dying then, I suppose. He was going away, too: he said so. 'I'll be a long time, Callum, lad. But it's going to be an interesting trip.' It was a trip that took him to the cemetery. Heaps of people from our family have made that trip. Guess I will, some day. Hard to believe.

I'd just taken a first step up the track when something incredible happened. I had this sudden thought. Yeah, yeah, it's incredible for me to have *any* thoughts.

Actually, I had two thoughts at once, which was *totally* incredible. But while I stood there, with the stick in my hand, one of my feet on the track, my mouth flopping open, I realised I was gonna remember this moment for the rest of my life.

I don't know if I can put it into words properly, but here goes. One part of my brain — the dim part — understood clearly, like it was reading from a whiteboard, that nothing is really new. Every person who'd lived in our valley, they'd all wanted to find something special, whether it was being happy or a success, or just knowing they belonged here.

But even though they wanted this something special, there was nothing special about the fact they wanted it. Hell, does any of that make any sense?

At the same time, the other part of my brain — the *really* dim part — was telling me something different.

While I kept standing there, foot in mid-air, stick in hand, mouth in flop, it was saying that everyone is special and so is everything they do. Any sense there?

I felt myself filling up with it. It was like when you come outside and stand in the sunlight on a really awesome day, and all this warmth and happiness comes flooding through you. The whole world seems magic; you can do anything, be anything. I can't ever say that sort of stuff to my mates, either!

I was going to live an amazing life. I was going to write, travel, be on the first manned mission to Mars if 50,000 other people didn't get chosen ahead of me. I guessed — I *hoped* — that lots of people before in our valley had felt the same sort of thing. That didn't matter. It was still my discovery. My treasure. *I'd* found it. Does any of *that* make any sense?

I began bounding up the track. There was a stupid grin across my face. I swung the stick in crazy circles; I heard myself laughing and half-cheering out loud. Hell, I hoped nobody in those flash new houses could hear me.

And while I was doing these weird things, these things that would get me locked up in a little white room if anyone saw, a third part of my brain — the one so dim it had been invisible up to now — clicked into action, and spoke to me. 'You've changed your mind about something else, too, haven't you?'

Yeah, I had. I was halfway up the track now, still leaping and sniggering and behaving like a happy psycho. Hey, if I timed things right I might even run into Marama driving Melody back.

I can write about all this, I realised, as I came skipping and jumping to the top of the track. All those people, with their stories; I just wish I knew every one of them. There's so much stuff, if you live here. So much (last time I'll say the word, I promise) treasure.

I had to tell someone. Mum and Dad . . . I stopped yet again as I began slinging one leg over the rails. What would I hear when I got back to the farmhouse? What had they decided? I wasn't sure what I wanted when I left there an hour and a half ago. But now I knew.

If I couldn't share it with them, then — a girl's face formed in my mind. Yeah, that girl. But I'm not mentioning her, remember?

A sound was coming from somewhere. A buzzing, howling sound, faint but getting louder. And getting closer. Someone else was flying a drone around? I shaded my eyes and peered upwards. Nothing, except for the hawk above the swamp.

Then two things happened at once. I dropped down onto the road at the start of the bridge. And the buzzing swelled into a roaring, as a car came rocking around the corner.

It was really hooning along. Stupid sods. After what happened to Aunt Maggie, didn't they realise? Plus there were so many farm driveways with milk tankers turning out of them, stuff like that.

Next second, my mouth flopped open again. The car wasn't just hooning; it was swerving from side to side, back end swinging so wildly that it almost ripped into the fence. It straightened up, hurtled towards me, swayed crazily once more. Smoke poured from the back of it. The engine was on fire!

Then I recognised it. The black car: the one with the two guys who had nearly run me down on the bridge. What were the morons doing now? I kept staring as they charged closer, motor roaring, the howling sound rising also. The car swung again, clipped a post, thundered on. More smoke billowed from the back.

No, not smoke. Something solid, shredding and spraying into the air. The rear of the car seemed to sag down onto the road. Sparks flew. Another burst of black, fountaining up above the roof, and I saw the remains of a back tyre go somersaulting into the ditch. The car raced on, fish-tailing as it came, wheel rim graunching along the tar-seal. I stood clutching the rail I'd just climbed over, stick in one hand.

It was only thirty metres away. And at that moment, the howling noise grew, and a police car skidded around the corner, lights flashing blue and red, siren shrieking. It straightened up and accelerated towards the bridge, gaining on the crippled black shape with every second.

The hoon car was almost on me. Through its tinted windows, I saw someone wrenching at the steering wheel, struggling to keep it straight. A last strip of rubber arced sideways into the fence. The whole vehicle slewed to the right, straight towards where I stood.

Next second, I was in mid-air, body looping over the top rail, stick in front of me, a pole-vaulter at some mad Survival Olympics. I'd never made a jump like this before. I could never do it again. I came thudding down on hands and knees in the rough grass beyond the rails, head twisted around to gape behind me.

The fleeing black car slammed into the side of the bridge, right where I'd been standing. Its doors buckled. The bonnet and boot crumpled and sprang up. Crashing and tearing sounds filled the air. I heard myself yell out. The car splintered its way along the timber side of the bridge for ten metres, bounced back into the middle of the deck, and was still.

I began to stand, then ducked as something else flashed into the corner of my eye. The police car, lights still flashing, siren cut off suddenly.

The front doors of the wreck flew open, window glass cascading and crunching from them. Two figures fought their way out onto the deck. One had dreadlocks; the other was shaven-skulled. They snatched a look at the cop car as it skidded to a stop. The shaven-headed guy yelled something that would have Mum grounding me for a week if I'd said it. Then he sprinted away along the bridge towards the far end. The smashed car half-blocked the deck behind him.

The one with dreads stared around. I could see his face twitching. Next second, he leaped for the broken railings that I'd high-jumped a couple of moments before, right above where I now crouched.

Blue uniforms were jumping from every door of the cop car. Voices shouted 'Stop! Police!' Hey, it was just like TV! Two of them — one was a woman, I saw — pushed past the wreck, and pounded off along the deck after Skinhead. Two others headed for the rails over which Dreads was clawing his way.

He threw himself down heavily, clumsily, landed on all fours just a metre from where I was hunched. For half a second, he didn't seem to see me. I made a gasping sound, and suddenly he was staring right at me, eyes slitted, face twisted. He'd hurt me if he had to; I knew it. He wouldn't hesitate. I shrank back.

The guy sprang up, started turning to leap down the track towards the riverbed. Above us, the cops were struggling over the rails (they weren't Olympic jumpers like me), still yelling 'Stop!'

Dreadlocks sneered, set himself to run. Even as he did so, anger rushed through me. Who did this guy think he was? How dare he invade and spoil this place that was so special, so precious to me and all my family?

My body flung itself forward. I swung the stick at him, smacked him across the back of one leg. It wasn't much of a blow, but it shoved him off-balance. He lurched sideways, yanking the stick out of my grasp, and half-fell, clutching at the grass.

He was up again instantly, snarling. He mouthed another word that would have had me grounded for a *year* if I'd said it, and chucked himself at me. I huddled into a ball.

He never touched me. Never reached me. The cops were there. One tackled him around the waist; the other grabbed his arms, had them up behind his back and the handcuffs on so fast that my mouth went into its flopping-open act again. Up above, I heard a distant screech and skid, as something happened at the far end of the bridge. More voices yelled. Hey, wasn't that—

Dreadlocks was struggling, glaring and swearing at me. But one cop grunted 'Don't be stupid, Zac. We've got you', and he sort of slumped suddenly. The second cop, a chunky, fair-haired guy, was looking at me, and at my stick where it lay on the path down to the riverbed. He nodded. 'Thanks, mate. Looks like we owe you.'

The two of them turned Dreads around, pointed him towards the railings. 'Up you go, Zac. No silly business.' The guy said nothing. All the aggro seemed to have drained out of him.

'They went straight through the road spikes and kept going,' the first cop told me, as we started climbing back onto the road. 'Stupid fools. Could have hit somebody.'

Yeah, me — like they almost had. But it was Aunt Maggie I found myself thinking of.

We were back on the bridge. My body shook; my breathing felt heavy, but I was OK. Both cops had a firm hold of Dreadlocks now, and that made me feel more OK.

A few metres away, the smashed black car almost blocked the deck. Its hot engine ticked and hissed in the sunny morning. Bags of green plants spilled from the sprung boot. Hey, wasn't that—? Yeah, must be. I felt angry again. Growing that stuff in our valley!

I saw something else, too. At the far end of the bridge, Marama's rural delivery van stood, angled across the road, its doors open so there was no way past. The shaven-headed guy lay spread-eagled across its bonnet, while the other cops, the guy and the woman, clamped handcuffs on him, too. Marama was halfway out the driver's door, watching them. While beside the front passenger's door, holding it firm and watching *me*, stood Melody.

The chunky, fair-haired cop slid into the police car; started talking on the radio. Dreadlocks stood, hands cuffed behind him, scowling at the ground. The cops at the far end of the bridge began marching Shaved Skull back along the deck towards us. Marama followed, a huge grin across her face, Melody beside her. A couple of cars had arrived behind the RD van where it blocked the bridge. People climbed out, and stood staring towards us.

'You all right, Callum?' Melody's nana called out as they got closer. The second cop who'd grabbed Dreads laughed. 'He's more than all right, lady. This idiot might have got away, if a certain young fella hadn't stopped him. Good stuff, mate.' I looked at the ground, too — but not before I'd seen the expression on Melody's face.

'You and my grand-daughter here are a real team,' Marama went on. 'We saw this guy tearing towards us, and the cops — police officers, sorry, constable — coming after him. I just gawped, but Melody went "Block the road! Block the road!" So I did.' She gave me a hug, then did the same to her grand-daughter. For a second I thought . . . but no. Not this time, anyway.

It took about fifteen minutes to give our names and cellphone numbers and my parents' address and stuff. 'Be someone out to get more details later, mate,' the policeman writing it all down told me. I liked his calling me 'mate'.

Two more cop cars arrived. Dreadlocks and Shaved Skull were taken away. A different cop was taking photos of the smashed black wreck and the bags of dope spilling from its boot. Other police were telling the growing queue of cars and trucks (I recognised Mrs Ross from up the valley and some others) that they'd have to take a detour, sorry. They wouldn't like that; it's an extra eighteen ks or so. Time we got another bridge in the valley, I thought. In *our* valley.

Melody's nana gave me a high-five. 'Work to do, eh? I'm late now, thanks to some guys capturing crims.' Melody gave me one of her smiles. 'See you, Callum.'

I tried to think of an incredibly cool reply, the sort you'd expect from a crim-capturer, and went: 'Aw, yeah. See ya.' One part of my mind announced that it wanted to kick another part.

She was turning away when she exclaimed 'Oh, look!' and pointed.

Upstream, in the shimmering air above the swamp, *two* hawks hung, side by side.

'Never seen that before,' Marama breathed. 'Never. Something special is going to happen, I reckon.'

Wrong. Something special had already happened. More than one thing.

I headed off for home. I felt different. Everything felt different. Man, wait until I told Nathan and my other mates about this.

The Waimoana glittered beneath the bridge. The whole valley felt like it was breathing slow and quiet in the sunlight. The names, lives, the *treasures* of all our family and all the other families who lived here seemed to be streaming through my mind.

I gazed towards the swamp once more. The two

hawks hovered there together, powerful and silent against the polished sky. A perfect pair. A real team, just like me and Melody. And all of a sudden, I had this picture of our two families stretching down through all the years, and of her and me, that . . . that I'll never in my life be able to tell anyone about. I whacked my crim-catching stick against the side of the bridge, and hurried on.

Over the stile, across the home paddock, through the gate. Dad stood on the lawn, staring in the direction of the bridge. 'Mum thought she heard sirens, son. What's all the traffic?'

Mum came through the back door, silver bracelet on her wrist. I saw she'd been crying, and something inside me seemed to turn over. They've decided, I realised. They've made up their minds. Nana Ailsa was behind, holding Pania's hand. The greenstone bat hung around Pania's neck, and there were tears on her face as well.

'Are you all right, love?' my mother asked. Uncle Sholto had followed the others out, looking serious. I glimpsed Great-nana Beth and Great-uncle John as well. 'What's been happening, Callum?' Uncle Sholto went.

I didn't answer any of them. I drew in a breath that felt

as if it filled my whole body. 'We're . . . we're going to stay here, aren't we?' I asked. 'Please can we — for ever and ever?'

David Hill lives and writes in New Plymouth.
His books for children and young adults have
won awards in New Zealand, the United
States, the United Kingdom, France and
Germany. His mother's family lived in a river
valley very much like the one in *Finding*.

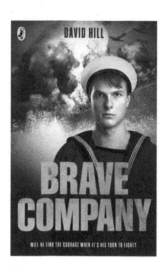

Sixteen-year-old Boy Seaman Russell Purchas is stationed on HMNZS *Taupo*, which has just entered hostile waters off the coast of Korea. It's 1951, and his ship is part of the United Nations force fighting in the Korean War. Russell is determined to prove himself against the communists — not just because he wants to be brave, but because he wants to escape the shadow of his Uncle Trevor, killed in World War II. Everyone thinks Trevor was a hero, but Russell knows the shameful truth.

But can Russell keep himself together when the shells start falling? And does he really know what courage means?

New Zealand Listener's 50 Best Children's Books List 2013

Also available as an eBook

. . . my right foot slipped on the accelerator. The engine revved, and the car shot forward. For half a second my eyes met Ash's. He was staring past me, through the windscreen. He began to yell something. Somehow I knew what it was. I wrenched my head round, foot stabbing for the brake. And there was the girl, right in front of us.

Tara is heading home. Ryan is driving his mates. Neither of them is paying attention. The tragedy that follows changes many lives.

Finalist, New Zealand Post Book Awards for Children and Young Adults, 2005

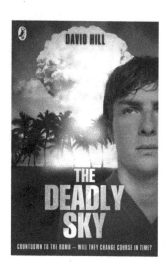

THE
DEADLY
SKY

COUNTDOWN TO THE BOMB — WILL THEY CHANGE COURSE IN TIME?

It's 1974, and a dark, cold New Zealand winter. So when Darryl's mum announces she is going to the remote Pacific island of Mangareva for work, and she's taking him with her, he is thrilled.

But even as Darryl soaks up the warmth and peaceful beauty of French Polynesia, his holiday is darkened by violent anti-nuclear protests. Plus there's Alicia, with her furious outbursts against all Pacific nuclear tests. Darryl knows she's talking rubbish.

What he doesn't know is that when he boards Flight 766 to fly home, his life and the lives of others will be changed forever.

Also available as an eBook

ENEMY CAMP

DAVID HILL

It's 1942, and the tiny farming town of Featherston is about to receive hundreds of Japanese soldiers into its prisoner-of-war camp. Ewen, whose dad is a guard there, can't stop wondering about the enemy just down the road. Some say the captives are evil and cruel and should be treated harshly — or shot. But when Ewen and his friends ride out to the camp to peep through the barbed wire, the POWs just seem like . . . well, people.

Then a new group from a captured warship arrives and the mood in the camp darkens. Guards and inmates begin to clash. As tension builds the boys are told to stay away. But on 25 February 1943, Ewen and his friends are there at the moment the storm breaks — and terrible, unforgettable events unfold before their eyes.

Finalist, Junior Fiction Award and Children's Choice Junior Fiction Award, New Zealand Book Awards for Children and Young Adults, 2016

Also available as an eBook

A gripping novel for young adults that captures both the daring and the everyday realities of serving in the Air Force during the Second World War.

Pete and Paul yelled together. 'Bandit! Nine o'clock! Bandit!'
Jack spun to stare. There was the Messerschmitt on their left, streaking straight at them.

Eighteen-year-old Jack wanted to escape boring little New Zealand. But he soon finds that flying in a Lancaster bomber to attack Hitler's forces brings terror as well as excitement. With every dangerous mission, he becomes more afraid that he'll never get back alive. He wants to help win the war, but will he lose his own life?

Also available as an eBook

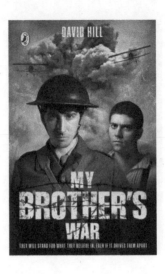

It's New Zealand, 1914, and the biggest war the world has known has just broken out in Europe. William eagerly enlists for the army but his younger brother, Edmund, is a conscientious objector and refuses to fight. While William trains to be a soldier, Edmund is arrested.

Both brothers will end up on the bloody battlefields of France, but their journeys there are very different. And what they experience at the front line will challenge the beliefs that led them there.

Winner, Junior Fiction Award and Children's Choice Junior Fiction Award, New Zealand Post Book Awards for Children and Young Adults, 2013

Also available as an eBook

Stuart and his twin sister Sandra are coming home to Wellington on the ferry. Stuart knows he'll enjoy the trip — he's a good sailor. But it's April 1968 and the ship is the *Wahine*. As the tragic events unwind Stuart and Sandra must battle to stay alive.

Winner, Children's Choice Junior Fiction Award, New Zealand Post Book Awards for Children and Young People, 2004

Also available as an eBook

Simon is a typical teenager — in every way except one. Simon likes girls, weekends and enjoys mucking about and playing practical jokes. But what's different is that Simon has muscular dystrophy — he is in a wheelchair and doesn't have long to live. *See Ya, Simon* is told by Simon's best friend, Nathan. Funny, moving and devastatingly honest, it tells of their last year together.

Winner of the Times Educational Supplement *Nasen Award, the Silver Pen Award and the Storylines Gaelyn Gordon Award for a Much-loved Book*

Also available as an eBook